Fireball: An Enemies to Lovers Romance

Lainey Davis

Fireball: An Enemies to Lovers Romance
By Lainey Davis
Join my newsletter and never miss a new release!
laineydavis.com
© 2022 Lainey Davis

Many thanks to Arwen Davis, Elizabeth Perry, and Yana
Ilieva for editorial input.
Cover by Dana Boulden, Creme Fraiche Design

Thank you for supporting
independent authors!

CHAPTER ONE
Samantha

I will sell this house today. I always channel Anette Bening in *American Beauty* when I think I have more on my fork than I can chew. *I will sell this house today,* I chant, symbolically referring to nailing an interview with a reporter from *Forbes* and meeting community leaders and all the other tasks that come with running a tech startup on the cusp of going public.

Forbes is just another interview. I've done a hundred of these by now.

Mirror check reveals my hair is looking fabulous. My skin has that peachy glow I get after a nice workout. Not a hardcore Pound workout with drum sticks—a nice stroll on the treadmill in the company gym before popping up to my office.

I check my watch. 7:55. Just a few minutes until my assistant arrives and just a few more minutes until the reporter strolls into my space. I lick my teeth and check the mirror again. Hearing a tap on the door, I turn my head, smile in place.

"Oh." I shake my head, seeing my CFO, Logan, and not my assistant. "Hey, friend."

She struts into the room holding a small bundle of yellow flowers. "Just wanted to bring you some sunshine before your big interview." She shrugs and sets them on my desk.

I look up at her, awed by the gesture. "That was really freaking nice of you, Logan."

She winks and pats the desk. "Knock 'em dead, Sam. I know you will!" Logan makes her exit and I pick up the flowers, giving them a sniff even though I know tulips don't really have a scent. I never know what to do when people do nice things for me like that, out of the blue.

It makes me uncomfortable, and I fully recognize that that's probably really telling, in terms of my mental health. I remind myself I've bought Logan flowers plenty of times.

Another tap on my door frame reveals my assistant, but she's not alone. It's go time.

"Morning, boss," Audrey says, nodding her head at the sleekly dressed man by her side. "I've got Mr. Childers here, from *Forbes*."

He flashes a toothy grin and I clench. I don't like this guy. My spidey senses tell me he's out to portray me in a bad way. But I'll win him over. I always do.

He hurries over to me with his hand outstretched. "Call me Isaiah, please."

I offer him my standard firm-grip-handshake. "Pleasure to meet you, Isaiah. Audrey, would you be able to put these in some water for me when you get a chance? I'd love to have them on my desk later." She smiles and gestures for the bouquet.

Isaiah starts talking. "So, Sam. Can I call you Sam?"

I hold up a finger for him to wait as I make sure Audrey gets what she needs and is on her way. Once she closes the door I sigh and put on my public smile. "Sorry. Hello. Sam is fine. Where should we start?"

He gestures around the room. "This is an impressive upgrade from a tiny dorm room."

I laugh the expected laugh and tell him about starting Vinea in my "spare" time in college, coding the software late at night when I should have been sleeping but needed to silence all the shouting in my head. Between the demands of my statistics degree program and my siblings calling me for all the things teenagers typically ask of a parent...well, let's just say I had a lot of anxious energy to burn off.

"Yes, I can tell you're very ... energetic." Isaiah thumbs through some notes. "So, you've compared Vinea to relationship management software? Tell me what that means."

"Vinea has become *essential* for a half million scientists worldwide," I tell him. "Our software is cloud-based. Do you know how many researchers were relying on paper? Emailing spreadsheets back and forth? Version control is a real problem, even for brilliant minds."

Isaiah frowns. "So it's an online version of a spreadsheet? For researchers?"

I shake my head, trying not to roll my eyes. "Vinea lets scientists track, measure and forecast their scientific work. There is so much repetition in labs, and researchers studying living cells...well there is just too much data to track and manipulate by hand. I know there's a problem in the world of life sciences research, and I know that Vinea can solve it."

A buzzing sound interrupts my train of thought and I look down to see my phone dancing across my desk. My brother's name flashes on the screen and I silence the call, turning the phone upside-down. "Sorry," I say. Isaiah nods. "As I'm sure you know from your prep work, my focus is tailored solutions for research institutions. Academic researchers use Vinea free of charge to track their work."

Isaiah nods again and holds a finger in the air. "I think I've read that you get people hooked while they're in school so they're dependent on Vinea once they enter the workforce?" He arches a brow at me sinisterly. My phone buzzes again and I slap the side button, holding it in and hoping this turns the damn thing off.

I smile again so I don't shake him. "While it's true I do

want my solutions to spread like a vine and dig their tendrils into every lab, I want to be clear that the scientists using Vinea aren't 'roped in' so much as they are transformed by how we can help them and their work. Think how much headspace these folks have to make sense of patterns and correlations once they have an accurate handle on the trends in their data."

The phone continues to jump across the desk, more insistently now. "Do you need to answer that?" Isaiah frowns at the phone.

"No, please accept my apologies. It's my family calling. I think they're just excited for me. You know, talking to such an important publication…" I try to stall as I succeed in turning off the phone. My family has no idea I'm talking with *Forbes* today. My brother probably needs help ordering new underwear and doesn't know his damn size.

"Isaiah," I tell him, trying to take back control of the interview, "in the past year Vinea has secured over $200 million in seed investments and we have a valuation of $900 million. My investors find us because all the life sciences companies in their portfolios adopt our solutions. Because biotech company leaders and entrepreneurs become accustomed to my software in graduate school. We believe this is the future of—"

The door to my office opens and Audrey pokes her head in, grimacing. "I'm sooo sorry, Sam. It's the Colonel on the phone. He says it's urgent."

Audrey hurries to take Isaiah on a tour of the building and I hope she catches my nonverbal cues and prayers to take him by Logan's office. Logan can charm even the slimiest of slime balls, and Isaiah seems none too pleased at being interrupted.

"I'm the CEO of a company," I tell myself. "A reporter should expect my time to be in demand."

I'm really good at appearing confident on the outside, when it's usually chaos in my brain. I take a deep breath and stare at the phone on my desk for another beat. The red "hold" light flashes at me insistently. I pick up the handle. "Hello?"

"Samantha." My father's sharp voice makes me shiver as if he were in the room to me, yelling at us Vine kids as if we were his soldiers. "I'm not happy to be making this call this morning."

"Well," I tell him. "I'm also not happy about the interruption. May I ask what's so urgent?"

"You did not send the notarized paperwork your brother requires in order to sell the beach house, Samantha."

I blow out a breath. I recall hearing something about paperwork but Audrey hasn't put anything on my desk recently. "I don't believe I received paperwork." I have to speak this way to my father, as if we are colleagues, rather than father and daughter. This is how he's always been, and this is how life was growing up with the Colonel at the helm of our family.

"I don't have time for impertinence, Samantha. Your brother has important real estate development on the line here."

I'm the CEO of an almost-billion-dollar company, I want to scream at him. *I have important shit I'm in the middle of, too.* But I can't say these things to my father and my brother is incapable of hearing them. My brother never remembered to actually send me the paperwork, and we both know it.

"Please tell Sean I'm happy to sign paperwork if I receive it," I tell him. "As you and he are aware, we have notaries on staff here at Vinea. I can and do handle these requests promptly. Now if you'll excuse me, I have a reporter waiting and I cannot take advantage of his time."

I'm able to hang up with my father only because there's another person's time to consider. I don't have to check my email to know I'll be receiving a frantic attachment from my brother's attorney. It'll be couched as a "resend" but the time stamp will show the real story.

And it won't matter. This will all just be another example of Samantha not doing enough to support the family in their time of need. My mother devoted everything to taking care of us, and when a pulmonary embolism took her from us in my teens, everyone just shoveled her responsibilities onto me.

I take another deep breath and remind myself that this is why I'm a terrific CEO. This experience is what has allowed me to squeeze more hours out of every day. I stand and smooth out my skirt, taking off down the hall in search of Isaiah.

"I'm soooo sorry, Sam." Audrey hurries up from her desk and starts to chase after me. "He was just so mean on the phone! I thought it was a real emergency this time."

I squeeze her arm. "You don't have a thing to apologize for, Audrey," I tell her. I know how my father speaks to people. "I'm sorry you had to field that call. Now, can you take me to that reporter so I can finish what I started?"

She smiles and gestures down the hall toward the conference room. I freeze, because I momentarily forgot that we invited all these people to come in today. My community relations manager said it would be good for Isaiah to see how Vinea gives back and builds partnerships, and make it easier for the reporter to grab quotes from people all at once. I can only imagine what Isaiah will try to worm his way into getting them to say.

I groan and then form fists, squeezing a few beats and releasing, trying to redirect all the energy flying around inside my body. Then I push open the door, stick a smile on my face, and head into the room, keeping my eyes fixed on Isaiah and his smarmy smile.

CHAPTER TWO

AJ

From: Vinelli, Kellie
Sent: Monday, August 28
To: [All Staff]
Subj: Morning Middle School Memo!

Good Morning Faculty! Who's ready for action?! We had a terrific first week last week!! Today we've got standardized tests in ELA so don't forget those positive incentives!! And let's not forget that AJ Trachtenberg will be representing Franklin Middle School at the Vinea Community Conversations meeting! Thank you, AJ!!! Can't wait to hear your report!
   Have a great day On Purpose!
   Kellie Vinelli, Principal

I don't care what my colleagues say. They sent me to this meeting because they didn't want to be here. See also: how I got chosen as science department head for Franklin Middle School.

You'll be a great representative for our kids, AJ!

You're the best one to remind all those folks about our

students, AJ!

Pure shtuss, as my Bubbie would say.

It's rough being a realist in a workplace where people overuse exclamation marks.

I sigh and straighten my tie, then reach for my folder and climb out of my compact Honda Fit.

Yes. I'm 30 years old and I drive a Honda Fit, even though I'm 6'-1". No, I don't think a man at my stage in life should be driving something flashier. No, I don't care that my sister drives a Range Rover.

I live in the city, I parallel park in the city, and I'll always choose fuel efficiency and dependability over prestige. I grunt at the haters who aren't actually here today and make my way inside the Vinea campus.

Who calls their workplace a campus? It's obnoxious, as is the perky person assigned to greet me, but I do accept the coffee they're holding out, because it smells amazing.

Hold on…yep. Tastes amazing, too. Okay, I will agree to release one layer of surly attitude in exchange for coffee this good.

"Let me just give you a quick overview of our campus." The greeter, a person whose name tag says Shane (They/Them), gestures to the left. "We've got all-gender restrooms throughout the building. There's a space out back for service animal relief if you need that, and we have a multi-sensory room on each floor."

It gets harder and harder to stay irritated with Vinea the more Shane lists the accessible features of their workspace. Pardon me. Their *campus.* I nod in thanks as they guide me to the conference room, snagging a coffee refill on my way in the door.

I thumb through the handouts for today's meeting. Community leaders from all over Pittsburgh were invited to sit down with Vinea to see how the company might be able to "give back." It feels like they want a tax break to me. I clench and release a fist as I remember my students. My seventh grade science students would love to see a space like this, to just be in the building and peek at computer scientists and their support staff.

I have to remember my students. Not everything is about me and my corporate cynicism. *Get it together, Adriel.*

I smile at the guy who sinks into the seat to my left and shake hands with him when he introduces himself as the leader of an organization that finds summer jobs and internships for teens in the city.

I nod and tell him, "I really hope Vinea can sponsor a few positions for you, man. This would be great experience for science-minded kids."

He nods back. "From what I understand, they agree to just about everything, as long as it's a good cause."

I scratch at my stubble, wishing I'd made more effort to shave today. Our principal said the same thing—told me to ask for anything and they'd probably give it to us. I'm just planning to ask for a field trip for the kids. Why didn't I think bigger?

Before I can dwell on it too long, the conversation around the table gets started. The Vinea staff are leading icebreakers while we wait for the CEO. Sam, the handout says, will be joining us for a "community conversation."

I try to focus on what folks are saying, but I'm distracted when the door pops open and a breathtaking, blonde-haired woman slips into the room. She's flanked by a scowling man in a suit and another Vinea employee, who waves at Shane.

"So sorry to keep you all waiting," the blonde says. "I'm Samantha Vine and I'm here to learn from you all."

Samantha—Sam. She is not at all what I was expecting, and that rattles me. I thought I had learned by now not to get attached to expectations. Shane starts leading introductions while I chastise myself for assuming the CEO was a man. I work really hard to overcome these sorts of preconceived notions. I take my role as a teacher seriously, and I take it even more seriously that I teach in a school district where more than 80% of my kids are living in poverty and food insecurity. My students deal with people's assumptions day in and day out, and I want to be one person in their life who wants to know them for who they are.

But also, this woman…she does not look like the CEO of a tech company on the brink of blowing up to the elite tier. This woman looks like a model. Someone who'd fit right in with Carnegies. From her perfect hair to her impeccable clothing, she's a picture of wealth and poise. Just like all the women in my past who've always judged me and made assumptions, had their own expectations based on wealth and status. Just like all the jerks who judge my students.

I feel my face scowling when Shane calls on me for introductions. They raise their eyebrows, gesturing at me to talk about myself, but I haven't been paying attention to what anyone else said around me, and I don't know if I'm supposed to name my favorite breakfast cereal or what. Best to cut to the chase.

"I'm AJ Trachtenberg," I huff out. "I teach middle school science for Public Schools of Pittsburgh. I'm sure you know we're under funded and we're always looking for companies to sponsor field trips for our students to enrich their—"

"Field trips to the museum?" Samantha interrupts me, one blonde brow arched quizzically as she asks for clarification.

"Well, no," I stutter, though field trips to the science museum would be amazing. There's never any money for *anything*. "Field trips *here*. For tours and job shadowing. So the kids can see data science in action."

She taps a pen on the desk and glances at the scowling man beside her. Who is that guy? "I'm not sure this is the best environment for your middle schoolers, Mr. Trachtenberg." She gestures around the room. "Our data scientists are working with very complex algorithms."

"And you think because my students live in poverty they can't comprehend what it is your employees do for a living?" I'm fully in a lather now. Peak surly. I take back my gratitude about the coffee. My lower back is starting to sweat. I hate when people underestimate my students.

"No," she says, shaking her head emphatically, causing some of the yellow waves to tumble over one shoulder. "Absolutely not what I meant. Perhaps I should clarify that—"

"Forget it." I slap my folder closed and cross my arms. "We'll just take them to Google." I realize this is an empty thing to say, both because we don't actually have a relationship with the tech giant and also because the companies aren't remotely the same.

It doesn't matter, though, because my words have the desired impact. Samantha Vine is flustered, stammering her way through the rest of the introductions as she assures everyone else in the room that Vinea strives to be a place where every voice is considered and welcomed.

Lip service. She's no different from any other money-hungry mogul.

As soon as the presentation wraps up, I leave my stuff on the table and stomp out to the parking lot. I don't even grab a third coffee on my way out the door.

By the time I get to the car, I feel like an asshole. I remember how welcoming Vinea's physical space is. I know I have a hair-trigger temper. But the fact remains that she doesn't want my students here, and by proxy she doesn't want me. I don't have time for people who don't want me in their space.   Not   anymore.

CHAPTER THREE

Samantha

The only thing saving me from curling in a ball and crying is the promise of meeting up with my friends. We call our little group Foof…Fresh out of fucks. It's a sort of ridiculous name for a bad-ass group of entrepreneurs, engineers and queens of the Steel City.

I feel so at ease when I'm with them, like I really don't have to pretend or put on a fake smile or any of that. I can actually free my fucks with these gals…and I need that, because everyone else claws at me, demanding attention I can't spare and hurling mean words at me if I say as much.

As often as we can, Foof huddles up in the event room of our friend Esther's bar, Bridges and Bitters, and these meetings are my recharge. Esther bought an old building in Lawrenceville and transformed it into the most amazing spot. She went for a speakeasy feel, with reclaimed wooden everything and these cozy settees. But honestly, we could meet on a milk crate by the river and I'd still walk away energized from these women.

A few days later, and I'm still reeling after I chased off Mr. Grumpy Teacher from our meeting and stumbled through the rest of my interview with the guy from *Forbes*. I definitely appreciate Esther's vintage velvet furniture as I collapse in a heap.

"That bad?" She arches a dark brow at me as she moves some furniture around the room to get ready for the rest of Foof to arrive.

I drape a wrist across my forehead. "If I had a corset on, I'd be asking you to slice the laces." She pats me on the shoulder and heads back up front to mix a batch of cocktails for us. My friends shuffle in, some of them excited about their day and others looking like they want to join me tying one on.

Logan links arms with her sisters-in-law as they make their way in. As they all chat about life, I sit up and rest my elbows on my lap, propping my forehead against my palms. "I wish I could have a do-over," I mutter.

"Tell me about it." Celeste Sheffield, actual grandma and the oldest member of Foof, sits next to me, patiently waiting for me to spill my guts.

I take a deep breath, thinking back over the wretched day, from the annoying call from my dad to my magazine interview not going well. I bite my lip, trying to decide the worst part of it all. "I told a middle school science teacher I didn't think young students would gain much from touring Vinea," I tell her. "So now this guy thinks *I* think his students are too stupid, because of poverty." Celeste pats my leg in a motherly sort of way I really appreciate.

"I was just so overwhelmed with the *Forbes* reporter there and thinking about how much work it'll be to prepare for going public. Who has time to prep for a bunch of tween visitors? But I guess what I said came out wrong and AJ took offense."

Celeste swirls around the ice in her drink and looks at me. "What if you called and explained? Said you realized your mistake? You could extend your invitation to the students after all."

I cringe. "Ugh. Apologies are the worst, though. Like, now this guy is going to know I say dumb things when I go off book." Men thinking I'm stupid is a big, fat trigger for me

13

after living with the Colonel. He's so domineering and immersed in a hyper-macho military world. Everything has to be precise with him. Language, thought processes, all of it. "Can I make Logan call?"

Logan laughs and shakes her head, wagging a finger at me. "I just run the numbers, boss. You're the one with your name on the building."

It's true. My name is on the damn building. So why do I feel like such an imposter all the time? I've spent my entire life trying to fill someone else's shoes...I got thrust into that role after my mother died. I didn't mean to start a company in my free time from my dorm room, but I did. Now, ten years along the way, I'm on the cusp of going public with my business-baby and I can't drum up the ovary power to call someone and apologize?

"Gah. Fine. I know, I know. I'll call him and grovel."

"That's the winning spirit!" Esther winks as she slides me a glass of something magical.

"What's this yummy drink?" I stir the liquid with the sprig of rosemary she stuck in the glass. Esther uses the Foof meetings to test out her new concoctions before adding them to her cocktail menu each month.

"I think I'll call this one Atonement." She waggles her eyebrows as she takes a sip. "It's tequila reposado, Amaro, lime, pineapple and some simple syrup."

"I only know what half of those mean," I tell her. "But it's damn good."

"Repent and find out," she tells me and shrugs. "Since when do you care what some man thinks of you?"

I always care. I bite my lip and look around the room. I can't let any of these women know how terrified I am of disapproval, of failure. No, that won't do at all. Gotta keep faking it. I'm a go-getter, damn it.

"Okay, okay, I'll call him. Sheesh." I take another sip of the drink, which is not quite a margarita, but is tart and sweet and smooth all the same. It tastes classy. Sexy. I stand up off the settee and wander into the hall. The quiet music Esther has playing in the bar creates a nice ambiance. It's loud enough that you can hear it, but still have a conversation with someone.

Like, say, a smoldering, grouchy science teacher I insulted earlier today...

I roll my eyes at myself for being nervous to call him and pull out my phone. Shane is a terrific manager of community relations, and I'm sure they sent me notes on everyone who was at Vinea today. Sure enough, there's a contact list in my inbox. They even made it clickable, so I just have to tap the name AJ Trachtenberg and the phone starts dialing.

It rings. And rings again. And rings some more. I take a sip of my Atonement. God, Esther really makes a damn good drink. Finally, the voicemail picks up and a low voice seems to growl at me. "This is AJ. Leave a message. I'm unlikely to respond."

I pull the phone from my ear and stare at it, hanging up before I can reconsider.

Was his voice that sexy earlier today? Or am I just drunk on Atonement? Who says that on their voicemail message?

I toss back the rest of my drink and set my glass on the bar. Gah. I have to call him again. But...then I get to hear his voice again... Should I waste my time leaving him a message if he doesn't pick up? Is this effort wasted? I tap redial and it rings ten more times. Ten freaking times before I hear the smooth baritone. The phone beeps at me, and I stammer into it. "Hi. Hello, Mr. Trachtenberg. This is Samantha Vine from Vinea. I was hoping I could talk to you about what we discussed earlier today. About your students. I mean, I would love to welcome your students to Vinea....You caught me a bit off guard earlier..."

I realize I haven't yet actually apologized, but can't decide if that's something I should even do over voicemail when he's unlikely to respond. I sigh. "Anyway, I'd appreciate a call back so we could talk about this further."

I hang up and slap myself in the forehead, groaning, before I walk back into the room full of my friends.

CHAPTER FOUR

AJ

I missed two calls last night. Nobody ever calls me apart from my parents and my Bubbie, so I never bother to answer my phone. I almost choked on my beer when I finally listened to the voicemail and it was from *her*. The blonde bombshell I happened to be Googling when I silenced her calls.

I'm not quite sure what to make of her wanting to discuss my students, so I decide to just ignore her call. We're dissecting frogs this week in my seventh grade science class. I have a lot to prepare and I don't have time to listen to someone else tell me about their incorrect assumptions about my students.

I wipe off my glasses, straighten my tie, and stride into my classroom, ready to face a room full of young teens who smell worse than the formaldehyde in the bins of frogs I stacked under the back window. "Morning, scholars," I say to my first period class.

They stagger in slowly from breakfast in the cafeteria, teasing each other, talking about football. I pull out my notes for first period and start arranging everything on my desk until a cracking voice interrupts me. "Yo, Mr. T."

I look up. "What's up, Dante?"

"What's the deal with the new art teacher?"

"What do you mean?"

"Well, like, how do I say his name?"

"Ah." I reach in my drawer for a dry erase marker and write Mx. Tran on the board. "Remember, their pronouns are *they and them*."

The bell rings and everyone takes a seat, silently waiting for me to elaborate. "And the M-x honorific is pronounced MIX."

Dante taps on his desk a few times. "Okay, but, like, isn't that weird?"

"Well, would it feel weird if I called you 'miss'?"

He laughs but then looks around. "Well, yeah. Cuz I'm not a girl."

"Right. Well Mx. Tran is non-binary. They are not a girl, either. Or a boy."

Jayden seems to ponder this a bit and raises his hand. "Doesn't someone have to pick, though?"

This is actually fitting in with my lesson plan about the reproductive organs in the frogs we're about to dissect, so I brighten up. "Glad you asked, Jayden. Let's make a list of all the things that make a girl and a boy." I draw two columns on the board and turn back to the class.

"Okay, who's got something for our list?"

"Boys have short hair," says Maya, a red-head with a long braid tossed over one shoulder. Another girl with a buzzed undercut turns around and says, "Yeah, but so do girls." She turns to face me. "Girls wear skirts."

Someone brings up the kilts on *Outlander*. The kids debate breasts and beards. We go back and forth this way for awhile, not settling on a single trait that seems to fit just one of the columns. Dante seems more confused than ever. "Mr. T, isn't this science class? What does all this have to do with biology?"

I grin and erase the columns from the board, writing "gonads" instead. I tell them to pull out their textbooks. We talk through the diagram of the frog reproductive systems, and I tell them how tadpoles sometimes switch sex before metamorphosing into frogs.

"Any given amphibian could be genetically male based on chromosomes, but have female gonads," I tell them. "Who can remember what we talked about with chromosomes?"

We talk through the different chromosome arrangements for a bit and I'm just about to pivot back to the frog diagram when Jayden interrupts me again. "Yo, Mr. T. There's someone at the door."

I look over my shoulder to find *her* standing there. Samantha Vine, leaning against my doorway with her arms folded, wearing the hell out of a pair of checked pants and a bright   red   top.

CHAPTER FIVE
Samantha

Does Steel-City Sweetheart Samantha Vine Have the Chops to Go Public?
By: Nick Ackerman, Business Analyst

Investors everywhere have one question on their mind this month as Vinea prepares for its IPO: when can I get in? The tech startup has soared to notoriety, enjoying nearly universal adoption from healthcare research institutions and biomedical companies alike. But is the company ready for the public stage? Moreover, is its leader prepared for the level of scrutiny that follows CEOs of publicly traded companies? Stay tuned as we follow the news this week on MarketView.

I don't have the heart to read the entire media summary Audrey pulled up for me this morning. I'm sure it's all the same thing each time: can I handle the competition in a big pond?

So, since I need a distraction and since AJ Trachtenberg never called me back, I decide to just pop by the school and hope I can catch him. I know it's a terrible idea, and probably disruptive. But the idea that he thinks *I think* something just hangs over me like a cloud. And besides—aren't kids excited about field trips? Even if he doesn't want to forgive my little misstep, shouldn't he just get over it to give the students a fun trip?

I also know that if I don't take care of this now, I'll get mired in a thousand other things at work and also stress out at the idea that my family might call me and yell at me for something else I didn't anticipate. Honestly, the weight of this thing with AJ Trachtenberg might be the straw that breaks my back this week. And I don't have time to find a spinal surgeon.

I approach the front doors of the school and ring the buzzer, explaining to the guard that I'm just here to talk to Mr. Trachtenberg.

I fumble my way through asking for directions to the main office until a guy in a button-down stops in his tracks. "Did you say you're here to see AJ?"

"Yes!" I brighten up at this ally, come to save me in the middle of my ill-advised mission. "I'm Samantha Vine. AJ and I had a bit of a misunderstanding yesterday at the Vinea event and I've been trying to track him down."

He holds out a hand. "Doug Rogers," he says. "Let me walk you up to his room."

"Oh. Won't he be teaching in there?"

Doug grins and nods. "He will indeed. I believe you will throw him off his game entirely."

I start shaking my head. "I can just leave him a note. It's just that it was hard to reach him over the phone."

"Sam. Can I call you Sam?"

"Please do." I love when people drop formalities. I grew up with a colonel for a father. I've had enough uptightness to last me a few lifetimes.

"Sam," Doug continues. "Nothing would thrill me more than to mess with AJ's head. He thinks he's unflappable and he drives the rest of us wild with that chip on his shoulder. Humor me, please. I've got three sons and I teach in a middle school." He grins and I can't help but like him. Apparently AJ

Trachtenberg is grumpy with everyone, not just me. Whew.

I shrug. "Show me the way!"

Doug leads me up a flight of stairs and points to a door decorated with cardboard microscopes and double helixes. Doug pushes the door open a few inches, grins and waves, heading back down the stairs as I lean against the doorframe to listen. AJ is really different when he's with his students. He seems animated as they talk about frog reproduction. I try not to laugh, remembering my own boring encounters with biology teachers. AJ seems passionate about his *students,* not just the subject matter.

Eventually, one of the kids notices me and I smile. AJ grimaces at me and I swear, he growls. Right there in front of his students, he growls like a wolf. Or maybe a grizzly bear. He's a very hairy person, I observe, noting dark strands on the backs of his hands, his neck, his jaw. I have to stop thinking about his jaw.

AJ says, "Class, this is Samantha Vine. She's come to judge your aptitude for science."

I frown. "Actually, I came to apologize. I didn't know I'd be disrupting your class. But I'd love to invite you all to my company, Vinea, for a tour. Once you're done with the frog gonads."

A girl raises her hand and says, "Mr. T, can we do whatever she's talking about instead of dissect the frogs?"

The class murmurs excitedly. Someone says, "Yeah, Mr. T. It smells like butt in here. No offense."

AJ just blinks and looks like he's grinding his teeth. The girl raises her hand again. He calls on her. "Yes, Margot?"

"Ms. Vine—what do you do at Vinea?"

I push off the door and walk into the room, grinning. "We dissect frogs." The class bursts out laughing and groaning and I wait for them to settle down. "Actually, I'm a data scientist." I look over at AJ to see if he seems like he'll murder me, but he's just quietly simmering off to the side, so

I continue. "I designed a software tool that helps scientists with their experiments. Have you all done experiments and lab reports and stuff like that?"

They all nod. "Okay, well, you know how you had to write down all your data and results each time? One of the things we do at Vinea is make an electronic notebook for our clients. They can keep everything in one place and also share it with other partners, even if those partners are far apart from each other."

"Can't they just email each other?" The girl, Margot, seems like she's ready to hear more about my work. Which I find energizing. I really regret saying no to AJ yesterday. Why did I let that reporter knock me off my game so much?

"Well they could, yes. But with our cloud based software, all the notes are in one place. And if people make them searchable, others might not have to repeat experiments that have already be done."

"So you made an online notebook?" Maya starts taking notes as I'm talking but AJ raises one dark brow at me, the other sinking low enough to nearly hide his dark, judgmental eye.

"Sort of," I say, hesitating. *Aha.* Here's where I was concerned initially about visiting with tweens. I don't know how to talk about my machine learning models that I built to make data entry standard and useful for all my clients, across industries. "When I was in college, my biology class was visiting a dairy lab. They were trying to study what to feed the cows to get the most milk. I saw that they were taking notes by hand, emailing each other...there were a lot of mistakes and there was no easy way to make sense of the data. To find patterns. So I built an algorithm, a computer code, to read over the data and notice things." I shrug. "At first it was mostly about helping scientists take notes. But I've added stuff since then as I built my team."

"What kind of stuff?"

I open my mouth to respond, but AJ chooses that moment to step forward.

"That's enough, Dante. We've got work to do here."

The class groans. I smile. "I promise to tell you all about it when you come visit. I'll set everything up with Mr. T."

Just then, he takes me by the elbow and starts walking me toward the door. I'm so stunned by the jolt of energy I feel shooting out of his fingers that I nearly trip. So then he reaches his other hand out to steady me and I'm surrounded by a crackling current. I think laser beams are shooting out of all his many hairs, just zapping me all over the place. I stare at him, realizing I'm hot for teacher.

Once we're in the hall, he gestures toward the stairs.

"Well," I look around, hoping Doug will materialize to save me again. "Are you going to at least call me back?"

He shakes his head. "I don't think it's a good idea."

"What? They were into it. I'll pay for everything. I know you said funding is an issue. I'll get Shane to put together a full day program and you can tell me if anyone has dietary restrictions and—"

"Samantha!" He uses his stern teacher voice when he says my full name and I feel it in every one of my nucleotides.

"Yes?" I whisper, shaking away the sudden fantasy I have of him rapping my knuckles with a ruler. I never even went to Catholic school, so I'm not sure where that comes from.

He rakes a hand through his dark hair, and a loose piece tumbles across his forehead. This man is a snack and he apparently hates me and that's a really bad combination, because now I'm fully immersed in a very deep desire to make him like me. Oh god, I'm seeking his approval.

"Look," he says. "Why don't I connect you with someone from the high school. Like you said, these kids are young for your kind of subject matter."

I shake my head. "I pity the fool who tells these kids they can't be data scientists." He raises a brow at me again. "Pity the fool? Mr. T? Don't they tease you about that all day?"

AJ rolls his eyes. "They're way too young for that reference."

"Really?" He doesn't respond. "Wow. So anyway, I was thinking about what you said during our brief, if unfortunate, encounter. And I'd love to spark inspiration for them. Give them an idea of some different career paths. Some of them might not even know—"

I'm interrupted by a shrill bell ringing above my head and the hallway is soon filled with teenagers, shouting, throwing paper at each other, and rushing past me like a current. I'm swept back against the wall.

"Maybe another year," AJ hollers above the din.

I shake my head at him, suddenly determined to get his students into my building, unsure if I need it for them to actually get inspired or if I am really this desperate for AJ to change his opinion of me. "I'll get you a bus," I shout, and then the students file into the classroom doors. Another bell chimes overhead. "Wow. That is really freaking loud."

He nods. "Yes. It is. Now, if you'll excuse me." And just like that, he spins on his heel and walks back into the classroom, slamming the door behind him.

CHAPTER SIX
AJ

By the time I swing through the teacher's lounge to grab my lunch, I've nearly forgotten that Samantha Vine interrupted my class this morning. I definitely am not trying to identify the unique blend of aromatics she uses in her cosmetics and I am absolutely not picturing her each time I bring up gonads with my students.

I will admit to being even more of a growling beast than usual when I see Doug leaning against the refrigerator, smirking at me.

"Had a visitor this morning?" He slurps his PM coffee like a man who doesn't care if it keeps him up past midnight.

"You brought her up to my classroom? In the middle of first period?"

"I did, yes." *Slurp.*

"Come on, Doug. There are protocols for these things. Does she even have clearances? Did you at least take her by the office?"

Slurp.

"Why are you like this?"

He sets the coffee mug on the counter and steps away from the fridge door so I can lean in and snatch my lunch. I yank the bag free and slam myself down into the rickety chair next to the photocopier. Doug slowly crunches a carrot, the sound of his chewing seeming to echo off the floor. Finally, he squints at me. "AJ. Are you suggesting I should have left the CEO of a wealthy tech company—who has tried to offer some financial support to our public school students—on a hard, uncomfortable chair in the office?"

"Yes!" I fling my hands out to the side, but bang my elbow against the copier in the process. I should have just kept my stuff under my desk and eaten my warm lunch alone in my classroom, where I could scroll through online cat videos in peace.

Doug shakes his head. "She said she is the CEO of Vinea, and I know for a fact you were there the other day to ask them to sponsor a field trip. And, as a member of the English department, I would have enjoyed a silent day here at the school, alone with my thoughts, if our students got to embark upon a scientific adventure."

I make a sound at him, one my colleagues have often described as a growl. "I'll find you a famous author your students can visit instead," I tell him, taking a huge bite of my sandwich. Cold meatloaf on white bread. Bubbie's finest. Delicious.

Doug snorts out a laugh. "Yes, because you run in the same social circles with famous authors." When I flip him the bird, Doug points a finger at me. "You know my wife's sister Alice married a Stag. And you also know Emma and Thatcher Stag do a writing and glass-blowing workshop with the kids every winter. We've got the arts all settled."

I actually forgot Doug's wife had that link with local celebrities. I could continue arguing with him just to prove a point, but I don't want to be petty. "Look, Doug, she implied our students aren't qualified to visit her precious space with her fancy coffee and there's no way I'm ever setting these kids up to feel less-than."

He arches a brow at me. "What did she say?"

I try to recall her exact words, and when I can't, Doug

jumps in again. "She came here in person to apologize. The CEO of a company in the middle of some very public business dealings. That means something, AJ." He shrugs and rinses his coffee mug before tucking it under his arm along with the remains of the bag of carrots. "Return her call. Let her woo the kids."

He walks out of the room just as two fellow science teachers bustle in. I nod my head at my colleagues as I continue eating my sandwich. Leo slaps a worksheet on the copier and then turns to look at me, smirking even more annoyingly than Doug. "Heard you had a visitor." He waggles his eyebrows.

"This is exactly like middle school," I mutter around a mouthful of sandwich.

Heather laughs as she waits her turn for the copier. "Duh, AJ. But seriously, who the hell scares off a community partner looking to sponsor a field trip? I heard her say she'd even pay for bussing."

I roll my eyes. "There's no way you heard her say that in the middle of a class change."

"Oh I heard it." She points one tawny finger at me. "You know damn well this school has to scrimp to provide soap in the washrooms. Why would you deny these kids a flipping field trip with career exploration opportunities? Go back to your hidey hole right now and call her back before the bell."

I sigh and set down my sandwich. "What exactly am I supposed to say to her?" I truly am hoping Leo and Heather have suggestions because when I think of talking to Samantha Vine, nothing remotely P-G comes to mind. And I can't set myself up for that sort of thing. Not anymore.

Heather rolls her eyes and holds up her hand, pretending it's a phone. In a mock deep voice, she says, "Hello? Ms. Vine? Yes, I can't stop thinking about your offer and I'd be delighted to take you up on it. If you could just put me in touch with your admin team, we can coordinate the details post haste." She mimes hanging up an old-school phone.

"Post haste?"

Leo taps his photocopies on the counter to straighten them and then hits me over the head with the stack as Heather steps up to the copier. "Come on, dude. Grow up. She apologized. She offered the kids a treat." He leans back and studies me. "Is that a new sweater vest?"

I nod and tug at my collar.

Leo nods his approval and Heather starts chanting, "Call her now. Call her now."

Eventually, I hurry out of the room just to get away from their meddling. They're right, of course. Everything about the Vinea building suggested that Samantha is a person who considers the needs of others. Whatever she said yesterday that set me off was likely more about me being sensitive than her being malicious.

And I am sensitive. Maybe I've always been, but definitely since my last breakup. I believe the phrase Leo uses is "frayed nerve." He keeps suggesting I see someone professionally. He's probably right.

I lock the door to my classroom and pull out my phone, scrolling through to my missed calls. I clear my throat and tug at my collar again as I hit the green phone icon. She picks up after 2 rings. *Shit.*

"Excuse me?"

"Did I say that out loud?"

"Is this AJ? Mr. T?"

I clear my throat. "Yes. Hi. Hello. I'm sorry I swore at you. I thought it would go to voicemail."

She laughs and I hate how much I enjoy the sound of it. "Well now we don't have to play phone tag. What's up?" It's like her voice strikes some sort of perfect frequency that lines up the cells in my body. Nope. This will not do.

"I, uh, well, thank you for your offer to treat the students to an in-depth tour of your facilities. And to provide transportation."

"Oooh, are you saying yes? This is terrific." I hear a clicking sound and imaging her typing a rapid email off to an underling while we speak. Must be nice to have underlings…although there are enough people in my life reminding me I could have underlings, too, if I hadn't chosen a life of "servitude." "What sort of time frame were you thinking?"

"I, uh, wasn't quite expecting us to work through the logistics right this minute." My collar seems to be shrinking in the afternoon heat. I keep pulling it away from my wind pipe.

"Hmm, well I'd like to settle as many details as possible right now to avoid unnecessary back and forth. Much more efficient if we just hash it out, right?" She doesn't give me time to respond. "You'll need time for permission slips and such, right? So let's look two weeks out. That's mid-September. How's the 17th?"

I shake my head. "No school that day. For Rosh Hashanah."

"Oh, really? It's late this year."

"You're familiar with Rosh Hashanah timing?" I'm not accustomed to people like Samantha knowing about Jewish traditions. I expected her to respond with some inane question about matzah. If I'm honest, I was hoping I'd get to tell her she had her holidays mixed up. It's much easier for me if the women I'm attracted to show me their flaws right up front, so I know not to get attached.

She continues talking. "Mm hm. Lots of my employees use their flex holidays in September for the Days of Awe. Okay, well, how about Wednesday of that week?"

Days of Awe. This woman knows the lingo of my people. I gulp. "I guess that's fine."

"Wonderful! And how many students do you have?"

By the time Samantha Vine is done, I've agreed to let her

team "craft" the permission form to include questions about dietary restrictions and access needs, and she vows to send a courier with printed forms by the end of the school day so we can distribute them at dismissal. She practically sings me off the phone and hangs up, leaving me staring at the phone in my hand as my fifth period students start jiggling the knob of my classroom door.

CHAPTER SEVEN

Samantha

Rather than work on the tasks I need to check off for Vinea's upcoming board meeting, I spend my time planning AJ's field trip. Which of course irritates Shane, because it's their job to work on this sort of community relations project. So they give me a talking-to, which I appreciate, and leave me alone in my office with binders and slide presentations to finalize.

Mercifully, my friend Chloe calls me, saving me from staring into space when I should be working. "Hi, friend," I chirp, remembering that today is a special day for her.

"Did you send me these flowers? These gorgeous, gorgeous flowers?"

Ah. I forgot I did that. "Well, yes. You deserve them. It's not every day my friend launches a book." I hear her take a deep sniff. "I don't really think ranunculus have a scent, chum."

"They're just so delicate and decadent. You really shouldn't have."

"Oh, knock it off. I can afford it and you're worth it and you said you were mentioning them in your book, so I thought it was a nice release day surprise."

"When did I say I put them in the book?"

I shrug and tap a finger on the desk. "One of the Foof meetings. A while back." Chloe writes historical romances, and they're equal parts spicy and mind blowing. She creates these characters who just feel so real, and I love how all her books end with everything happy. Not just the love part, but all the siblings get along by the end and everyone feels fulfilled professionally, too. Her books are the juiciest fantasies I've ever encountered.

"Well, I've got your signed copy right here, as per usual."

I smile at that, imagining adding the colorful paperback to the shelf in my living room. I don't ever read physical books anymore, but I love having copies of Chloe's books. I've got our friend Emma's books, too. So many Foof members are out there producing amazing things. It makes me that much more determined to succeed with Vinea. "I'm really glad you called, Chlo. You snapped me out of a funk."

"Well, I'm just floored that you remembered to do something nice for me even with everything you have going on." I don't tell her I set a reminder in my calendar for the day before all her book launches so that I get a card out to her at minimum. I know she's dealing with some sadness that her husband doesn't really seem to celebrate her book releases, so I just want to make sure there's one person who knows her in real life, that's rooting for her. Chloe sighs. "What's the next step with your I. P. O. thingy?"

I groan. "Well, Logan handles most of all that, thankfully. I'm waiting for the fact checks for the magazine article, though. I can't shake the feeling that the reporter is out to portray me as a ditz."

"You're the furthest thing from a ditz I've ever known. Wait. That sentence is weird. My brain is fried."

"Go drink champagne or stare at your flowers or something. I gotta get back to my data cave."

We say our goodbyes and hang up and I stare at my monitor some more. I really can't afford too much time with my thoughts unmoored like this. I take a deep breath and pull up my calendar, thinking I can just look at the week ahead and maybe settle on what I need to be doing. Each day is a rainbow of appointments and reminders. Red for Foof meetings or Foof-related reminders. Green for Vinea meetings and deadlines. Ah, there's a blue one for Mom's birthday.

She'd be turning 60 tomorrow if she had lived. Twice my age. In another universe, I'd be busy planning her a kickass party. You bet your butt I'd get ranunculus for her, and any other flower she wanted. I tamp down the sadness creeping in as I realize I don't even know what sort of drink she'd love to be sipping as I sat her on a glistening throne, wearing a shimmery boa.

"Nope," I say, closing the lid to my laptop and standing up from my desk. "This isn't going anywhere." I drive myself to Esther's bar, knowing I should confide in my friend that I'm feeling my grief today, but also knowing I probably won't tell her this. Nobody likes a downer.

Before I go in the door to Bridges and Bitters, I pull up my phone and make a donation to the American Heart Association in my mom's name. That's better than dwelling on something I can't change. Feeling slightly more upbeat, I make my way inside and grin when I see the place is packed.

There must be some sort of sportsball event happening. This city goes nuts for its sportsball, although sporty people usually go to sporty bars to watch games and things. Maybe Esther has finally reached a level where she's packing people in on a random Thursday. I shoulder my way up to the bar and see her simultaneously pouring drinks and offering instructions to another bar tender, who's trying to keep up.

I stare at them for a bit, transfixed as they work in unison, and then I feel someone staring at me. I turn my head and frown when I identify the hard, dark glower of Mr. Grumpypants himself. "AJ Trachtenberg? What the hell are you doing in my happy place?"

His eyebrows shoot up, like he's surprised I recognized

him. Okay, maybe he's taken aback by the vehemence of my words. But it is not okay for him to be here right now. This is my friend's bar, where I come to smash the patriarchy. Where I'm supposed to open up about my dead mom, or not, depending on the vibe I get from Esther.

I shake my head and slap the bar. "Esther, what's going on in here?"

"Hosted a training session," she mutters. She doesn't even look up at me as she keeps stirring and pouring, her strong arms whipping around bottles like she's a machine. I feel compelled to figure out a way to make things more efficient for her, to help her streamline this process somehow, but I feel a sharp poke in my upper arm, yanking me back to the present.

"Are you following me?"

Is he seriously asking me this? He looks serious. Shit, he looks good in his teacher clothes, all dark and growly. "Why would I be following you? And why are you so mad at me?"

Esther slides a drink into my hand at that moment and I don't bother to look down at it. I bring the glass to my lips and stare at AJ, waiting for him to explain himself. Why *is* he mad at me? Only my family gets mad at me. Seriously. People love me.

AJ looks at my hand and my drink. "So you just happen to be here tonight? When there's a professional development session for science educators?"

I take a big sip of my drink, smacking my lips in response to the tarty blend of amazing flavors. "AJ. This bar, this mixologist…these are my things that I do with my spare time. I am not here to pander to science teachers. But seriously why are you mad at me? Is this because I came to your school?"

He runs a hand through his hair and sighs, taking a pull from his bottle of beer. He should have let Esther choose something for him to drink. I bet a stiff drink would wipe that mean smirk off his face. The crowd around the bar thins out as people acquire their drinks and make their way toward the tables and booths.

I rest a hip against a stool and stare as AJ slides into the adjacent seat, still staring at me with one brow raised. "You shouldn't have come to the school. But if you did, you should have waited in the office and not interrupted my class."

"Your friend brought me up to your class. I would have been perfectly happy to sit outside the principal's office and wait."

"I would have made you wait for a long time."

I roll my eyes. "There you go again being mean. You really do have a Mr. T temper."

AJ barks out a laugh, surprising us both. He takes a quick drink to hide his frustration at being amused by something I said. "I should get back to my group," he says, looking like he can't decide which is worse: staying next to me or returning to the other science teachers, who are staring at him from across the room.

I wave. He glowers. "Well don't let me keep you," I tell him, and he huffs away. I barely even stare at his ass.

"You gonna tell me more about that whole situation?" I turn to see Esther leaning against the bar, grinning at me.

I hook a thumb back over my shoulder. "That's the guy who I was awkward with at Vinea the other day, so then when you all advised me to call him and apologize, he wouldn't answer his phone."

"Oh lord. What did you do?"

I bite my lip. I hadn't expected Esther to take his side in all this. "Well. I went to his school to apologize and reiterate my offer to give the kids a tour and a nice day. I've even lined up some data scientists to do some activities with them. Wait til you hear about it. We're giving them access to the software and designing some little learning games for them. It's going to be a whole thing."

"So he was already upset with you, and you went to his

workplace unannounced, and now you showed up at a work thing he's attending at my bar?"

I hand her my empty glass. "I guess none of that is technically incorrect."

She rinses the glass and puts it in the sink behind the bar. "Well. He's looking at you like he can't decide if he'd rather fuck you or run you over with his station wagon."

I turn around and see that AJ is indeed looking at me from across the room, an unreadable expression on his dark face. I think his stubble grew in a little more since he walked over there. Is he really irritated because I invaded his space? This just makes me more determined than ever to win him over. I love a challenge, and there's nothing more challenging than trying to make a grouchy person happy.

When I turn back to face my friend, she laughs and shakes her head. "I can feel you plotting from here, Sam."

"Well what would you do if someone didn't like you?"

"Lots of people don't like me." She shrugs. "That's their problem."

"Hmph." I fold my hands on the bar and try to remember why I came down here to begin with. I guess it's a successful visit if it distracted me enough to temporarily forget. "I'll win him over," I tell her.

Esther laughs and starts washing glasses. "I'm sure you will."

CHAPTER EIGHT
AJ

"You want to tell us what that's all about?" Leo grins at me as he takes a sip of his beer, the smug jerk. I roll my eyes at him as I settle into my chair across from Nathan Cho, a science teacher from a neighboring district. The two of them do not look like they want to debrief about the training we just attended regarding online alternatives to dissection for students who conscientiously object.

"The blonde doesn't look like a teacher," Nathan says.

I frown at him. "'The blonde' is the founder and CEO of Vinea." I practically grunt my defense of Samantha.

"No shit?"

Leo nods and elbows Nathan. "She dropped by the school the other day to apologize to AJ about some misunderstanding. Because he didn't call her back."

"Ooh, she called you? Dude, why wouldn't you lock that down?"

I take a long swig of my beer, draining it, and I set it on the table with a little too much strength.

Leo scratches at his chin. "I bet this is about Lara." He turns toward Nathan. "AJ's witch of an ex. She fucked him up in the head."

I don't even like hearing her name, and I resent having my almost-fiancee brought to my consciousness. Maybe it's not fair to even think of her as my almost-fiancee, since she was pretty clear our future together was all a figment of my imagination. *How could you honestly think I'd* marry *someone like you, Adriel?*

Shame and embarrassment wrestle for dominance in my guts and I shift in my seat uncomfortably at the memory. Eventually, I realize Leo and Nathan are staring at me with slightly softer expressions. "Hey," Leo says. "It's been like two years. You gotta at least go have your rebound fling."

Nathan taps his beer bottle with his wedding ring. "I've been out of the game a long time, but I'm pretty sure it's not even a rebound at this point." He and Leo turn around to stare at the back of Samantha's head as she talks to the bar owner, who apparently actually is her friend.

"Quit staring at her. Come on!"

They slide back around in their seats. Nathan sets his empty drink on the table and rises to his feet, stretching. "Well this has been invigorating," he says. "But I have to get home to the other Mr. Cho." He shakes open his jacket and slides it on. "Don't let the tech lady wait too long. You've got her number? Use it." He whistles as he walks out of the bar and Leo nods enthusiastically.

"What he said, man. Come on. It's like fate, her following you to school and then showing up here. This city isn't that small."

I start to cycle through all the excuses I give my parents and my Bubbie for why I haven't been dating since my love life exploded, landing on, "She's not even Jewish, Leo."

He seems to consider this for a beat and then shrugs. "Well, Lara was a nice Jewish girl, right? That didn't work out so well for you." I wince. He holds up a hand. "I'm not trying to be harsh, AJ. It's just that it seems like you're working awfully hard to come up with a reason not to dabble in some romance."

"Dabble in some romance? Where do you even come

from? And besides, that woman is insufferable."

He leans forward, pinning me with a dark, mischievous grin. "I'll tell you what. Either you try to make something happen or I'm going to go full Italian Stallion and see if she's looking for a good time."

"Leo! God, can you not objectify every woman we encounter?"

He chuckles and runs a hand through his dark hair. "She's a beautiful woman, AJ. I'm a single man. We already know she's smart. I can think of worse ways to spend an evening than taking her out for dinner."

At his mention of worse evenings, I try to suppress the dread I feel each day after school when I return to my apartment, which I've still not rearranged after Lara left. Every evening is a reminder of what I no longer have, what I never really had to begin with. Sparse furniture, only a few mismatched dishes. What once seemed minimalist and fiscally responsible, I now see through Lara's perspective. My evenings are austere, below society's expectations. Subpar. Women like Lara expect a certain lifestyle, and that lifestyle is not compatible with the public school teacher whose parents chose lives of service rather than riches and glamor.

My family has money—old money, Lara would say. There are entire wings of medical schools named for the Trachtenbergs. My parents bucked the trend to open a neighborhood clinic, and supported me when I switched my major from pre-med to science education. My college girlfriend on the other hand...Lara thought my interest in teaching was a phase I'd outgrow.

I'm not going to get burned a second time. Samantha Vine is like a blonde, waspy version of Lara, all smiles and friendly speeches...until she realizes there's no significant nest egg, there's not going to be a luxury car, and there won't be a restored Victorian in the east end of the city, let alone a

McMansion in the suburbs. Leo and I stare at the back of Samantha's head. "She's out of my league, man," I say to Leo, shoving the table away from me as I rise to leave.

Leo reaches for my wrist and looks me in the eye. "I keep telling you, AJ. You've got it wrong. *You* are out of Lara's league. And Madam CEO over there would be lucky to have a guy like you."

I shake my head and yank my hand free from his grasp, leaving the bar without looking back. I find my car and, even though it's out of the way, I drive through my childhood neighborhood. Someone is setting off firecrackers, as per usual on nights when it doesn't rain. I pass the small building that houses my parents' medical clinic, looking shabby and stucco as it always has.

I think often of my father, who earned his medical degree at Vanderbilt and chose a family health practice in a clinic that supports patients with limited resources. He found my mother, a woman who also values making a difference over making a fortune. It's super cliched that she's the nurse in his clinic, but the two of them love their life together.

They're out there every day, diagnosing diabetes in the "pre" stage and curing people of chlamydia and all I ever wanted to be was just like them. *Someone like you,* Lara said the night she upended my life.

I cross from Greenfield into my new home in the Squirrel Hill neighborhood, where I can walk to both my grandmother's condo and our synagogue for services. I thought moving to a neighborhood with a larger Jewish population would be a concession for Lara, where we'd do great and humble things but live among the wealthy peers Lara values so deeply.

Someone like you.

I snort at the memory and growl, "Never again!" I squeeze my Honda into a tight spot outside my building and head inside, determined to keep Samantha Vine out of my thoughts.

CHAPTER NINE

AJ

"Okay, hear me out." Doug leans against the counter in the teachers' lounge, munching baby carrots as usual.

"Whatever you're about to say, I hate it."

"My wife wants me to come with her to a book thing."

I shrug. "You love books. You're an English teacher."

He groans. "Yes, but this is a romance book release thing. Amy said there will be some other men there, but I was hoping you'd come along."

"You want me to come along with you on a date with your wife? To a romance book event?"

He nods. "Yes. I'd like you to keep me company while my wife swoons. Maybe you meet another swooning woman...plus I will owe you."

I arch a brow. "Owe me what?"

He holds his palms up. "Name your price. Recess detail? School dance chaperone?"

"Wait. I have to chaperone the dance? Since when?"

Doug waves a hand, dismissively. "AJ. Please?"

I sigh. This sounds like the absolute last place on earth that I want to be...apart from alone in my empty apartment, I guess. I act like a huge jerk about it, but Doug is a good friend and a solid colleague. We've taught together since I was fresh out of student teaching. I groan. "Fine. Text me the details."

And that is how I find myself under-dressed at the Fort Pitt Museum, surrounded by people in 18th century costumes, gushing over the historical romance talents of romance author Chloe Petals. This party is like someone wanted a re-do on their bar mitzvah, with over-the-top decor and costuming only the ultra rich can pull off on a weeknight. Doug and Amy are nowhere in sight and I scowl as I dodge women in huge skirts and bonnets with giant feather plumes that tickle my nose.

I wander up to a table with stacks of books on it. *Rebel Heir* appears to be the sequel to *The Redcoat,* in which a colonial woman falls for a British soldier. And then they have a child. Who apparently grows up to be the hero in this next bodice ripper.

As soon as I form the thought of the words *bodice ripper,* I turn to see a heaving bodice. Samantha Vine stands beside me glaring, with her hands on her costumed hips. She's dressed in a low-cut blue gown with a bow in between her breasts, and I cannot draw my eyes away.

"What in the hell do you think you're doing here, Trachtenberg?" She hisses at me and snatches the book from my hand, slapping it back on the table and shaking the stack.

"Maybe I'm here to meet Chloe Petals," I growl back at her. "What's it to you?" This woman gets my goat every time, and we seem to be running into each other everywhere. If she's not insulting my students or disrupting my class, she's galavanting around playing dress-up.

Samantha snorts. "As if Chloe wants you here. You're not even in costume." She pokes me in the shoulder and I stare down at her lace cuff. It flutters as she breathes heavily at me.

"If you must know, I'm meeting a colleague and his wife."

She shakes her head. "You're impinging. You keep showing up at my events with my special people."

I arch a brow at her. "This is your event?"

Samantha rolls her eyes. "I'm throwing this party for

Chloe, yes. *Someone* has to champion her and her amazing writing."

I open my mouth to retort but I feel a hand on my shoulder. "God, AJ, so sorry we're late. Amy had an issue with her dress." I turn to see Doug in a long wool coat and tri-corn hat, which he doffs at Samantha. "Good to see you again, Sam."

She purses her lips, like she really can't believe I was telling the truth about why I'm here. Recognition flashes across Samantha's face and she seems to compose herself. "Doug Rogers, right?" She offers him her hand like some English lady and he actually kisses her knuckle, earning him a swat from his wife.

"Oh, sorry, this is Amy. Aim, this is Samantha Vine."

Amy's face lights up. "Oh, you're from that Foof group, right? Alice loves hanging out with you." Amy is dressed as a bar maid and I try to avert my eyes from her bosom, which leads me to stare back at Samantha's. I swear if that bow moved, I could see her nipple. I cannot be standing here in jeans thinking about Samantha Vine's nipple.

By the time I compose myself, Samantha and Amy are gushing about Sam's friend group, and Doug has grabbed my arm. "We can just ease away now and find the bar."

As we step inside, I swat Doug in the stomach. "You didn't tell me it was a fucking costume party."

He cringes. "I only found out an hour ago."

"And it didn't occur to you to call me or something?"

His eyes widen. "I did call, man. Your voicemail message says you don't take messages." He shrugs and reaches into a metal bucket, extracting two plain glass bottles of beer. I sigh and take a swig. I look around the room, which is mostly full of women fanning themselves with copies of *Rebel Heir*. There is just one other man that I can see, dressed as a colonial soldier, complete with a fake musket. At least I hope it's fake. He's got his arm tightly wound around a woman who is talking animatedly to... "Aw, hell."

Samantha whips her head to the side at my words, seeing me again. She strides over to Doug and me. "You're like a child," she says. "Following me around. I have enough people in my life trying to con their way into my free time."

"Look, I don't know what your problem is, but I'm just trying to drink a beer with my buddy here." I elbow Doug, who is mid-sip on a beer and spills some on his cravat.

"Shit," he says. "I gotta go find some paper towels or something. This is a rental." He rushes off toward the bathroom as Samantha's eyes flare at me.

"I hope that doesn't stain."

"Well, lucky for him, he's friends with a science teacher. I've got tricks that can get stains out."

Samantha furrows her brow. "Okay, that's actually pretty useful." We stare at each other for a few beats and I will myself not to look at her chest. It doesn't work. It's all I can do not to reach out and cup those full globes. I squeeze my beer bottle with both hands.

A woman steps up to the podium at the front of the room and taps on the microphone a few times, causing the guests to wince and then hush. "Hi, everyone," she says, nervously. "I'm Chloe Petals." Samantha lets out a whoop that sets off a round of applause. "I just want to thank you all so much for being here with me tonight, to celebrate my new release. I can't tell you what it means for me to have home-town support." She sniffs. The crowd claps again.

Chloe points a gloved finger toward Samantha. "I would be remiss if I didn't acknowledge the extraordinary support of Samantha Vine, the most amazing friend anyone could ask for. I know that sounds generic and I'm a writer so I should be able to do better." Chloe sniffs again and blows Samantha a kiss. "I'm just thankful is what I am. All of you, everyone who reads my books, makes it possible for me to keep on writing them."

A dark-haired woman in the crowd yells, "Chloe, we love

you!" I recognize her as the bartender from the other night. What did Samantha call her? Expert mixologist? I really am intruding on Samantha's social circle, and I don't understand how that keeps happening. I don't socialize with this type anymore.

Chloe opens a copy of the book and begins reading from a chapter apparently set around the Treaty of Paris. I note that Samantha is watching the crowd rather than Chloe, a look of pleasure on her face.

I step closer and lean in to whisper, "It was nice of you to do this. Host a party for her."

She turns to face me, her eyes shining with emotion. She seems to struggle to think of a comeback and eventually just nods. "Thank you," she says.

By the time Chloe finishes reading, Doug has returned from the restroom looking none the worse for wear. Samantha drifts away and Doug studies me. "You want to hate-fuck her," he says. I don't bother denying it.

CHAPTER TEN
Samantha

I hate that I have to attend a weekly calendar meeting with my staff, but I accept that such a thing is part of being the person in charge. That doesn't make it any easier to pay attention to Audrey as she details all the investors coming in to Vinea to chat with Logan and all the places Shane needs to go to discuss community relations.

I miss holing up in a room with my computer, three monitors blinking at me as I code furiously, chasing down the rush of a successful program that meets its objective: streamlining something important for people. Making their lives easier.

I sigh and look up at the screen, where Audrey is talking through the color-coded map of leadership obligations. Logan is in her element, syncing up links and bios for each executive in real time, attaching all the pertinent info to each calendar entry. I'm so glad I poached her from that shitty investment firm where they were treating her like crap.

I smile and admire my leadership team as they sit there, thriving. But, soon, it's time to hear my list of responsibilities. My job has shifted so dramatically since I built my flagship software product. I used to jump out of bed with a busy mind and tinker with code. The first time I sent my program to another researcher, waiting to hear their opinion of the program was exhilarating. Like riding a roller coaster. The flurry of amazing text messages I got in response? Felt like one of the loops halfway through the ride, when you're over the nerves and just loving the weightless experience of inertia.

"Mmm," I say by accident, causing the team to turn and look. "Sorry. Was waxing nostalgic for a minute. Tell me more about this keynote address I'm delivering."

Audrey folds her hands in front of her and leans toward me. "I hope the rest of the team will support me in saying I think it's time we brought in more support."

The room fills with murmurs of agreement and I look around. "What sort of support?"

Shane raises their hand. "Marketing and communications, please! We have to stop outsourcing to an agency. You need someone in-house and you need to stop writing your keynote addresses yourself. All due respect," they pause and I nod, gesturing for them to continue. "A pro can come in here, whip up company emails, spruce up our web copy, talk to the press, and bang out a speech for you and it'll feel like you wrote and said it all. I'm serious."

I bite my lip. I'm friends with writers. I'm no stranger to the impact of good professional communicators. I'm just upset that it hadn't occurred to me that we needed that here at Vinea. Well that's not true. I always feel this desperate need to do everything myself. Who else can do it as well as me? Then I cringe, because I look around this table at all these people I love who are amazing at their jobs. I groan, suddenly worried our tremendous growth hasn't been as well thought out as I assured the public. "What else do we need? Don't hold back on me, team."

They all start speaking at once until Audrey grabs a dry erase marker and starts taking notes on the walls. I'd forgotten the conference room had walls we could write on. That must have been Audrey's idea. Soon, we have a plan in place to hire a vice president of business strategy, a communications director, and a few others whose titles I frankly don't understand. But I trust Logan and Shane and Audrey when they say we need them.

I don't love the idea of conducting this many executive job searches in the short amount of time before we go public. I start to panic a little bit, worrying that we should have had this sort of team in place long before we started accepting the level of investment we're getting.

There are only a few minutes left in the meeting when we get to the calendar item I was most looking forward to discussing: the Franklin Middle School field trip. I perk up as Audrey reviews the plan of action, starting with the swanky chartered bus picking up the kids, continuing with the amazing breakfast and lunches we're bringing in for them, and culminating in a bunch of hands-on activities we set up, including some coding workshops and fully loaded touch-screen tablets for the school to keep.

Logan figured out that if we donated all this stuff to the school PTA, we didn't have to go through all the red tape of having the school board approve the tablets, and soon she and Shane are engaged in a technical battle of wits about fiscal and community responsibility. Audrey uses the opportunity to lean in to me and whisper, "did you happen to see that your dad's birthday is next week, too?"

Crap. I swallow. "Yep, thanks Audrey, I've got it all in hand."

I do not have it in hand. I haven't made restaurant reservations anywhere, let alone made travel accommodations, bought a gift, or wrangled up my siblings for a celebration the Colonel won't appreciate anyway. I'm going to have to charter a damn private plane if I want to be here for the field trip and also make it home to Virginia.

Logan and Shane agree to disagree about something and the meeting adjourns. I retreat to my office to figure my shit out before I have to meet with a research hospital CEO. "Okay," I say to the empty room. "This is fine." I pull out my phone to call my father, who answers after one ring.

"Colonel Vine speaking."

"Hey, Dad. How's your day going?"

"Samantha I don't have time for casual conversation."

I close my eyes. "Noted. Have you given any thought into how you'd like to celebrate your birthday?"

He pauses and I clench my teeth together. This could go so many directions, and I really wish I could predict which it would be. My father is like a computer program I can never crack. He's not predictable, except that his actions are predictably unsettling. Eventually, he says, "I anticipate my children organizing a suitable celebration."

Of course. And by "children," he means me, because I'm the oldest. So, obviously, I'm meant to take on the full burden of organizing the meal and the gift so that my siblings aren't inconvenienced by my "failure to plan ahead." We went through this routine when Dad turned 50 the year I was launching Vinea while simultaneously attending school full-time with a double major in statistics and computer science. God forbid my brother or sister call a bakery or a restaurant.

I shake my head. That's defeatist thinking and I need a growth mindset here. "Of course, Dad. I was just checking if you had a particular restaurant in mind. Or an experience! My friend Orla just took her dad on one of those pedal bar rides. It looked so fun, the whole family riding around sipping some suds…"

"We have open container laws here in Virginia, as you well know, Samantha."

"Right. Anyway, I'll call up the trattoria like usual. Six o'clock, right?"

"That is the standard time dinner is served."

"Okay, well, I'll probably meet you there since I'll be traveling from my office." I hurriedly wrap up the conversation before he can realize that I'm not taking a day off work to travel down there and spend quality time with my siblings.

I fumble around my desk for a piece of paper so I can write "CALL DAD" and then cross it off with flourish. I realize I own a tech company and could do this electronically. Sometimes the physical act of marking off a list feels cathartic. I decide to add CALL SEAN and CALL SARAH. And I add an H to her name just because I know it would piss her off if she saw it. I also know I'm not going to call her. She hasn't spoken to me in years apart from absolute essential communication at holidays. I'll send her a text after I give Sean his marching orders.

I manage to quickly book the restaurant online and order a small cake from my favorite bakery here in Pittsburgh. I figure I'll just bring it with me on the flight, which I'll have to book later. I've just about got myself psyched up to call my brother, when Audrey taps on the door. "Crap," I say to her. "It's time for the hospital guru, isn't it?"

She nods. "Remember, she's Belgian, so all the parts of her name have a French pronunciation."

I squeeze her arm. "I appreciate you, Audrey. Always making me look good." I stand up from my desk, smooth out my skirt, fluff up my hair, and walk away from chores that make me groan, toward a meeting that should fill me with energy.

Except I'm not quite feeling this meeting. I know the whole thing could be a quick email. Most research hospitals are already using Vinea in their labs, and sharing data across studies at different institutions. Our program makes it easier for labs to collaborate as long as they all have the right permissions. Of course, Vinea has the permission forms and International Research Standards built in as clickable options. My meeting today with Madame Dubois-Devos is just a formality. Yet instead of feeling excited to shake hands with someone else who loves my work, I feel unsettled.

As I walk with Audrey to the door, I decide it must be because my father was once again emotionless. I plaster on a smile and drum up my best French pronunciation as I greet my   guest.

CHAPTER ELEVEN

AJ

"This bus is sick, yo." Maya and Jayden run their hands along the smooth white exterior as they stare at their ride for the field trip. Leo stands beside me, chewing complimentary pastry noisily in my ear as the students file onto the massive, gleaming double-decker bus parked outside the school. Vinea has somehow set up a breakfast cart on the curb, with smiling servers keeping up with the masses of Franklin students clambering for croissants and cold-pressed juices.

Leo elbows me in the ribs. "She sent food for the whole school, you know. Not just the kids going on the bus."

"Mmm." I grunt at him, fidgeting with my clip board, suddenly wondering if I'm under dressed again for *this* adventure in a shirt, tie, and sweater vest. The bell rings for first period and Leo starts wrangling seventh graders inside the vehicle. I climb inside and am hit with a fresh scent. The air doesn't smell like bus air at all. The temperature is cool, the ambient music is soothing, and the driver grins at me as I make my way to the top level to count students, who are all beside themselves stroking the leather arm rests and adjusting their overhead lights.

Margot raises her hand and I nod at her. "Mr. T…this is amazing."

I nod. "It's really something."

"Mr. T?"

"Yeah, Jayden?"

"This company has fuck-you money."

The kids burst out laughing and I take a deep breath, reminding myself they are young tweens exercising their independence. Margot grimaces, and says, "They must be rolling in ice if they can casually send this sort of stuff for us."

I nod at her. "Vinea is on the brink of becoming publicly traded on the stock market. Do you all know what that means?"

Margot and her classmates shake their heads. The kids I grew up around talked about investments at the breakfast table. My students rely on the school to provide their breakfast. "Well." I fidget with the clipboard again. "We'll go over it in a little more detail later, but let's just say your first impression is pretty spot on, even if your language is crude."

Eventually, with all students accounted for, I head back down to the first level of the bus, where Leo pats the seat beside him, smirking. "I heard that." He takes a sip of coffee.

"How did I miss the coffee? I only saw ginger carrot juice."

Leo hands me a coffee and winks at me as I inhale it greedily. I can't hold back the moan of pleasure. I need to find out where Vinea orders their coffee and start ordering these beans by the bushel. "AJ, I'm just saying, there might be another explanation for why CEO Vine would roll out this kind of bling." He emphasizes each syllable of CEO with a fist pump.

I raise a brow at him, too blissed out by the coffee to engage him with proper sarcasm.

"She could be trying to impress you." My eyes widen at him. "She could be trying to get in your pants." He pops the P in pants and nudges me with his shoulder. The bus lurches forward and the students all start applauding before I can tell him he's being ridiculous.

All morning, as the kids are treated like royalty, I should be focused on the career readiness information Samantha's staff is presenting for the students, but I can't get past Leo's suggestion that this decadent, wet dream of a field trip might in some way be an effort to impress me. *Someone like me.*

I remember my first interaction with Samantha at the nonprofit thing and decide it's possible I misjudged her. Although, come to think of it, we haven't seen her yet today.

Shane, who I remember from the last time I was here, is breaking the students into groups to test out Vinea's software programs. Once Shane sends the kids off with various Vinea employees, I pull them aside. "Hey," I say and they smile.

"Mr. Trachtenberg," they say, extending a hand for a shake. "I remember you from our nonprofit summit. I'm delighted to build this partnership with our public schools!"

"Oh." I never know how to respond to enthusiastic people. Even before Lara ripped my emotional guts out I was more of a silent observer than a gesturing shouter. "Well, this is indeed terrific for the students. But I was wondering…" I can't believe I'm both asking about the whereabouts of the CEO and nervous about doing so, but here I am. "Are we going to be seeing Ms. Vine today? To thank her, you know, for the hospitality."

Shane smiles wider. "She's meant to drop in on one of the sessions later, yes." They lean in conspiratorially and whisper. "She's having a very, very dramatic week, though, so I didn't want to preview that for the students in case it doesn't work out."

"Oh, of course," I say, nodding. I remember how I told Margot the company was on the brink of going public. And I remember how the Vinea CFO explained that process for the middle schoolers while also highlighting the ways finance and math can fit into careers in STEM fields.

This entire fucking day is basically our principal's fantasy.

Samantha Vine is showing these kids a future they could grasp and giving them contact information for mentors who want to help them get there. And why shouldn't she. Isn't this why I teach? To offer opportunities and epiphanies to young minds?

I wander out the door into the hall, intending to check in on one of the student groups, but I catch sight of Samantha through the windows of a conference room. She's pacing and clenching and releasing her fist, passing the phone to her other hand and repeating the motions. She looks more like she did the day I met her, like she's on the brink of exploding. I think of how casually she leaned on the door in my classroom and dropped dissection jokes, how she tossed banter at me at the bar like it was nothing.

I wonder which is the real Samantha. I can just make out her words as she paces by me and I hide my face behind a pamphlet. "Sara, do you think it's fair of you to say that to me? It's reasonable for an adult to chip in for a parent's birthday gift...I'm not asking you to pay for the meal...Of course I didn't ask if you were available tonight. Today is his birthday. I also am not available tonight, but I'm making it work...I'm not rubbing anything in your face. I have to get back to work."

I watch as she slaps her phone on the table and takes deep, heaving breaths. I watch as she smooths out her skirt, like she's preparing for battle rather than leaving the battle. She opens the door, and I expect her to approach me or Leo or the students, but she breezes right past us down the hall.

Two men in designer suits stand holding folders, eyebrows raised, expecting something. "Gentlemen!" She beams at them. "So sorry to keep you waiting. Please make yourselves comfortable and we can go over the paperwork together."

I don't like the disappointment that rolls through me as I realize I'm not going to get to talk to her. Not for a while at least. And then I force myself to stop thinking about it. I walk back into the room where my students are navigating an online program used by the world's most prestigious scientists and research institutions. And I feel proud seeing how well they understand the concepts and the scientific terminology.

By the end of the day, Dante and Margot have both proclaimed they will be applying for summer coding camp scholarships and the rest of my students have already figured out how to link their new tablet devices together to join worlds for a massive Minecraft game. Shane informs the students there is wifi on the bus, and I've never seen middle schoolers file back into a coach so quickly in all my years as an educator.

We're about to close the doors and shove off when a blonde blur comes rushing out the sliding glass doors of the Vinea headquarters. "Wait!" Samantha swings her way into the bus and leaps up the staircase. She stretches up toward the top level and then squats down to wave at the ground level. "I hope you all had a terrific day," she says and smiles as the students all cheer. Beside me, Leo also cheers. I glower at him, inexplicably, and he shrugs. "I so wish I could have spent more time with you but I know we'll meet again when you all apply for summer internships with Vinea, right?"

When she winks, I think every human on this bus falls in love with her. I worry about the reaction I'm having in my pants as she tells the students how to access her contact information in the tablets they all received, and encourages them to "at" her on social media. With a final wave, Samantha pivots off the bus and rushes back inside the building. As the bus pulls away, I watch her staff descend upon her, each person waving papers and vying for her attention.

"You've got it bad, amici." I realize I'm leaning across Leo to stare out the window, and I feel myself blush as I sit back in my own seat. "You should ask her out. I'm telling you."

"Does she look like someone who has time to go on a date with a middle school teacher in a sweater vest?"

Leo punches me in the arm. "She'll make time when you ask her."

I spend the rest of the ride back silently stewing, angry with my friend for leading me down a line of thinking I've tried to suppress. No more fancy women who want fancy things. I've done that already and I've got the emotional scars to prove it. Samantha Vine can have her swanky company with excess riches and amazing coffee.

I'm fine over here with my family, my work, and my students. "Shit," I murmur as the bus pulls up outside of the school. "I forgot to ask where they get their coffee."

CHAPTER TWELVE

Samantha

Vinea Launches Sweeping Search for Candidates in Key Roles
  By: Chip Tulley, Inside Business Reporter

Recruiters are cracking their knuckles this week as Vinea launched a series of high-level job searches to fill roles in communications, Human Resources, and corporate strategy. Inside Business noted postings on various job boards, all emphasizing a desire to locate diverse talent to quickly fill roles as the company prepares for a public option later this fall. Does this broad job search indicate trouble at the helm of the tech startup?

"All right, hit me." Audrey falls into step with me as I make my way back to my office. She's got a stylus in hand, ready to cross things off her electronic agenda. I wish I'd thought to use that the other day when I was angry-listing. I experience a minor wave of concern that my piece of notebook paper wound up in unfriendly hands, but I don't have time to dwell on it, not with Audrey beside me. She explains how Shane hired a recruiter specializing in inclusive hiring and Vinea already lined up prospects for a few key roles.

"We've got the candidate for communications tomorrow.

The strategy specialist candidate asked to come Friday, but I said we need to move to next week since you can't spare an hour two days in a row."

"That sounds smart. But ugh. Can I really not spare an hour on Friday?" I look at her hopefully and she shakes her head.

"Okay, so I know you need to leave for the private air strip in a few minutes, but I really need you to approve these forms for the S.E.C."

"S.E.C sounds like a Logan situation. Isn't that for money stuff?" I have zero mental capacity to concentrate on money stuff at this point in my day.

"Logan has already signed." Audrey looks at her notes. "She says, 'tell Sam to go for it. Everything's in order. I got you, babe.'"

I arch a brow at Audrey as I reach for the pen she's holding out while we walk. I pause to lean on the wall. "Did Logan really add that last part?"

Audrey nods and gathers back the signed forms. "She did. Okay, in your office you'll find gals from the investment bank Logan selected. They want to talk with you before moving forward. They know you have a hard stop in—" Audrey checks the time. "Seventeen minutes. Give me your phone so I can charge it during the meeting. My intern is finishing up packing your bag."

"I'm not staying overnight."

"Oh, I know, but we thought you might want to change for dinner or just have some comfy things for the flight back. We've got you, babe."

I press open the door to my office and look over my shoulder. "When did you get an intern?"

An hour later I arrive at the airport, having spent the entire car ride with Shane and Logan talking me through the finer points of our price stabilization plan and community members who want to join our board of directors prior to the public stock offering. I don't even get a chance to check my texts before I have to hand my ID to the pre-check security person.

Audrey follows me on the plane and for a terrifying moment I'm worried she will be coming with me to Virginia to tell me more things I need to think about and I won't have a minute to prepare myself to "enjoy" my family. But she just hands me my phone and pulls me in for a hug.

"I know they're mean to you," she says. "But I want you to know we all love you here. We appreciate your amazing work."

I feel tears well up, but I don't let them spill. I don't have time for that. Haven't in years. "I'm moved, Audrey. I hope you all know how much I value you." She gives me a thumbs up and backs off the plane. An instant later she shoves her hand out as the flight attendant is about to close the door.

"The cake!" Audrey's other hand starts waving the pink bag containing my father's sugar-free birthday cake. I lean forward to grab it from her and when I clutch the bag to my chest, I see that someone stuck a cupcake in there.

A green sticky note on the wrapper says SAM, and I moan in gratitude as I greedily peel it open and cram the decadent chocolate into my mouth. My staff is amazing. I can't believe I put them in a position to all feel overworked, just because I couldn't let myself cede more control of the company. Audrey, Shane and Logan really push me. I need to compensate them better.

Energized, I pull out my phone and refuse to allow myself to groan or frown as I scroll through the messages from my family. My *happy birthday* text to my father shows as read, although there's been no response. That's par for the course.

My brother has repeatedly texted to ask where the dinner will be and what time. His final message reads, "Nvrmnd I found it."

Also par for the course.

I put my phone back in my bag, opt not to change clothes,

and spend the rest of the flight speed-reading all the briefs and memos from Shane, Logan and Audrey. I start to wish I had a co-CEO and will myself not to get my phone back out to look up whether such a thing exists.

Once again longing for the late nights just making coding magic happen, I prepare for landing. I know Audrey arranged for car service to and from the airport and I look out the window, laughing as I notice we are sharing space with the military planes. In another universe, I could hop in a Jeep and share a ride to dinner with my father. The proud Colonel could show off his daughter, the one whose software is (as of two days ago) being used by military researchers.

I try to imagine how I might bring such a thing up to my father, that my company has secured military contracts. It's been so long since we've talked about anything other than my brother's bright future…

Outside the restaurant, I catch sight of said brother, who nods silently in greeting. I notice he is not carrying a gift bag. He doesn't seem like he's got a birthday card in his jacket pocket. "Hi, Sean," I say and I wait for him to pull the door open, since my arms are full with my carry on and the cake. Sean pulls out his phone to check something and I have to clear my throat and say, "A little help?"

"What? Oh." He reaches past me and opens the door. I breathe long and slow through my nose, approaching the host stand.

"Vine, party of four," I say with my best smile.

The young woman at the podium looks up at me nervously. "Some of your party has already arrived," she says, in a tone that suggests my father got here early, and is upset that the rest of us are not also early. I follow her around the corner to the window table, which glows in light from a charming candle arrangement and a soft pink light fixture above. Dad doesn't like to eat in places that are too dark, because he likes to be able to see both the menu and his food.

When I made the reservation, I asked them to keep the house music low and the lighting a little higher, at least in the area where we're seated. I turn to the hostess. "Thank you so much for your attention to our special requests," I tell her. The pinched look on her face eases up a bit. I look at my father, who is concentrating on his crossword puzzle. "It's 5:58, Dad. Almost time for your birthday party!"

I slide into the chair across from him. "Oh. Hello, Samantha." Dad checks his watch. "Cutting it a bit close, are we?"

I pat his hand. "Not as close as Sara, right?"

Sean rolls his eyes and Dad looks at his watch again. "I don't think we should be expected to wait for her if she's late. Do you know what you'll order?"

Sean huffs out a laugh. I pat Dad's hand one more time. "The server hasn't even brought menus yet."

"We eat here multiple times a year, Samantha. I think you know what they serve."

I shrug. "Maybe I feel like duck today. Or fish. We don't always have to get the same thing."

"Well, I will be getting the same thing." He looks over his shoulder. "I'm glad some places know to keep the racket down with the background music. I like to hear myself think."

This is as close to a thank-you as I'll get from my father.

A few moments later, the host hustles back to the table with my sister, who is wearing all black and a scowl to match. It's been years since she's spoken to me unnecessarily. I know that she's actually mad that our mother passed away, but it's getting harder and harder to be the person who bears the brunt of my entire family's grief in that regard. I miss Mom, too.

"Happy birthday, Dad," Sara says, sinking into the seat by his side. I can't decide if it's more awkward to have to sit across from my sister or if it would be worse to be next to her, my shoulders rubbing against the angry, black fabric covering her angry, black soul.

Our server arrives with the menus and asks if we'd like to hear the specials. I open my mouth to say yes, but Dad cuts him off. "We all know what we want already," he says. "I'll have the chicken, my son will have the pork chop, and both my daughters like the scallops."

The server blinks a few times and looks around the table as if to confirm. I weigh the pros and cons of standing up for myself and asking for a god-damned minute to read the menu, to choose what food I eat at the dinner I planned and will pay for. And I decide to nod. I start calculating the number of seconds remaining before I can leave.

Dad looks at my brother. "Sean, why don't you tell your sisters about the progress you're making with your real estate investment. Now that all the appropriate paperwork has been received."

I close my eyes and drink from my water glass, vowing to at least buck tradition and get a glass of wine with my meal, despite what my disapproving father thinks. Sean begins to toss around developer slang as I feel my phone buzzing in the bag pressed against my calf under the table. Slowly, painstakingly, I lean to retrieve it without drawing attention to myself.

I glance at the screen to read the preview from Audrey. *Just a reminder to write your keynote speech for the science educators event.* I let the phone slide back into my bag and pat my brother on the shoulder as if I've been listening the whole time. I'm not sure when I stopped trying to get him to look up from his own navel. At some point I just realized I couldn't make him be kind or considerate of others.

I think about Audrey's message, about a gathering of science educators. Someone comes to refill our water glasses and I grab his arm. "I'd like a glass of your house white wine, when you get a chance, please." I smile brightly at him as my father scowls.

"Samantha, really? You can't go one night without imbibing?"

"It's a party, Dad. I'm going to have a glass of white wine with my scallops."

He grunts. "Sorry, Sean. Please continue."

My brother looks like he's jealous, even more so when the server slides the cool glass of wine into my hand and I take a satisfied swig. "Anyway," he says, "I'm pretty excited about the net cash flow…"

I stop listening, sipping my wine, smiling into my glass, and thinking about grumpy AJ Trachtenberg sitting at a benefit dinner. If I'm speaking there, he'll have to look at me. I think about how it will feel to have those dark eyes burning through my soul as he stares.

"Samantha, is there something you'd care to share with us?" Dad has his arms crossed, frowning at me.

"Oh. Sorry. I was just thinking about work."

"About your computer stuff?" Sean tries to reach for my wine and I move it out of his reach.

"We landed a military contract this week, and I'm feeling really excited about this use of our software. It's a fantastic opportunity."

My siblings and my father just blink at me. They have no idea what I do and they don't ever ask me to elaborate on it. Often, if I talk about work, they scold me for boasting. It must sound jarring for them to hear that my "little college side project" has grown to this sort of magnitude.

"Which military contract?" My father scratches at his chin, contemplating. I know the work he does centers mostly around the troops and strategy, not research.

"Obviously I'm not allowed to talk about the particulars," I say as my sister's jaw drops. "But Army biomedical researchers will be using my software to track their projects and ease collaboration with their partner universities." Nobody is interrupting me, so I take a sip of wine and keep talking. "You know, the military has a beautiful, unparalleled data set for the healthcare of service members, since they all use ServeCare. They have anonymized data about absolutely everything, so it's been a real gift to sync up the database with all the functions of our programs."

Sean squints at me. "I thought you made video games or something?"

I turn to glare at him. "Why would you think that? I've never even played a video game."

He shrugs. "You started doing all this in college. Don't college kids just sit around and play video games?"

I bite my lip, considering how best to respond. "Vinea makes lab work easier, more reliable, and recreateable. I know you all think I'm just bragging when I talk about work, so you might not be aware that I have built partnerships with every major medical research institution in the country, now including the U.S. military." I shrug. "I did think of the idea in college, yes. But I am now CEO of a corporation. And we form legitimate partnerships."

Dad purses his lips. "Well." He nods. "It sounds like we're keeping you from your work."

You are! I want to scream. *You didn't ask me what worked with my schedule and you never ask me anything about myself, my needs, or my feelings.* I want to tell all of them that I want them to actually want to spend time with me, and not because they want me to do something for them. That all I've ever wanted from them is a hug and to hear that we're all in this together.

Instead, I say, "I'm happy to be here celebrating your special day, Dad."

By the time the server brings my scallops, my wine is gone and my enthusiasm is completely drained.

CHAPTER THIRTEEN
Samantha

I dig into my carry-on bag in the back of the car, yanking off my heels and sliding my feet into the soft ballet flats the mysterious intern packed for me. I squeal when I find a pair of sloth-patterned pajama pants and slide those on underneath my skirt, which I then shimmy off as we coast through the light traffic en route back to the private runway.

By the time I reach the jet, I've transformed from respectable business maven into a sloppy Abercrombie model…with a killer bag. As soon as the flight attendant tells me I'm allowed, I whip out my phone and start up a video chat with the Foof group.

Only Chloe and Esther answer, and Esther is back lit from the bar so she's more of a fuzzy presence. "My family is so miserable," I tell them.

Chloe mimes giving a hug. "I forgot today was the big fancy birthday party."

I roll my eyes. "The Colonel got judgmental when I ordered WINE. One glass!" I hold up a finger to the lens.

Esther leans close to the screen. "What did they serve, do you know? Was it any good? I'd kill to find out their profit margin on a house wine."

"I did not take the opportunity to ask for the sommelier," I deadpan. I groan and let my head drop back on the headrest.

"I'm surprised how good the connection is from your fancy

airplane," Chloe says, munching on something white and flaky.

I tilt my head to stare at her. "What on earth are you eating?"

She holds it up to the screen. "It's hard tack. I made it myself. I'm doing research."

"Hard tack?" Esther fake gags and then steps off screen to pour a drink.

Chloe nods. "My next hero is going to be a lowly soldier and not an officer or anything."

"Oh my god, Chlo, please don't go full method and give yourself scurvy trying to write about hunger."

She shakes her head. "I promise, I won't. But hey. You look like you need a hug."

I nod. "I really fucking do. Work is just bananas right now. All I wanted to do today was hang out with those kids on the field trip at work but I had to take meetings the whole day. The whole day!"

Esther pops back on screen, one eyebrow raised. "Field trip? Am I hearing that you spent time today with Professor Pout?"

"Who?"

Chloe claps her hands. "That's what we're calling your grouchy crush. Esther says he liiiiiikes you."

I roll my eyes. "He can't stand me. Which, as you know, is a huge trigger for me. Nobody hates me apart from my own family, damn it!"

"So you didn't win him over yet?" Esther laughs and leans her elbows on the bar. She must have me propped against a tap.

"I didn't even have a chance to talk to him. But I'm sure he'll be excited about our debrief conversation tomorrow."

"You're gonna de-brief him all right. Even if he wears boxers!" Chloe snorts.

"Good one, Chloe." Esther gestures to give her a high five

through the screen.

They tease me for a few more minutes before Esther gets slammed with customers and Chloe's husband comes home from work. "I gotta go try to talk to him," she says, crunching the last bite of her hardtack. "See you at the next Foof meeting?"

"Wouldn't miss it," I say as she hangs up. I wonder if she realizes how truly I mean those words, how very vital it is for me to be there with people who listen to me, who see me, who notice all the ways I try so hard. Without my Foof ladies, I drown in the voices of my family. I need my friends in Pittsburgh to help me remember what's real.

I feel that choking, sweaty approach of tears and I shake my head rapidly. I reach in my bag to see what else the intern shoved in there and purr in delight when I find a bag of apple chips. "I freaking love these things," I mutter, reaching in to the crisp, cinnamony treats.

My mom used to pack these for outings because they were so light weight. I remember her doling them out to me and my siblings. She made her own, I think, dehydrating them in the oven in our on-base housing. I love that Audrey and the intern knew to stick them in my bag for a treat.

Nestled below the apple chips are Shane's notes about the field trip. I smile at their neatly typed bullets about community awareness and their plan to ask one of the teachers to join the Vinea focus group.

I wonder if they're thinking of inviting AJ to the group. I sort of doubt it. The two of them didn't hit it off when they first met. Not that I hit it off with AJ, either. I chuckle at Chloe's joke about de-briefing him. He definitely seems like the sort of guy who wears plain white briefs beneath those neatly pressed teacher-slacks.

Why doesn't he like me? I was obviously frazzled in that meeting when I initially said we weren't a good fit for a middle school field trip. I sigh, thinking about all the wisdom

I've ever heard about first impressions.

I suppose I don't have time to worry about AJ Trachtenberg and his early notions about me. I'm on the brink of a public stock offering. I have meetings from sun up until sundown, and then I have shit to read all night to prepare for the next day's meetings. So why can't I get him out of my head?

The plane lands in Pittsburgh and I feel overwhelmed for a moment, not sure what comes next. Did I drive my own car to the airport? How am I getting home? Thankfully I see a woman waving a sign with my name on it and I take a few minutes to marvel that I've become one of those people who has a professional driver meeting her at the airport. With a sign and everything.

I step into the back seat of the car, laptop fired up, ready for the evening's reading all snuggled in my sloth pajamas. And yet my thoughts keep drifting to a pouting science teacher and all the ways I want to make him approve of me.

CHAPTER FOURTEEN

AJ

"You're late." My Bubbie hefts herself into the front seat of my car, tucking her skirts inside so I can close the door without getting grease on her good clothes.

"Nice to see you, too, Bubs." I climb in my side, grinning, and lean across to give her a kiss before pulling out for the short drive to our temple. It would be faster to walk, by the time I find parking, but Bubbie has been complaining about her hips recently, so here we are.

"No kippah? What is this—Sunday school?" She clucks her tongue at me until I lift the console compartment and pull out the battered old yarmulke I keep there for just this sort of emergency.

"I just forgot, is all. I couldn't find my keys this morning. I was running a little behind."

She shakes her head and pats my hand on the gear shift. "You're never going to find a nice girl in a wrinkled old head covering like that, Adriel."

"I thought we go to services to find peace. Nobody said anything about ladies." I wink at her.

Bubbie crosses her arms and studies me for a few minutes until I pull up outside the doors of the synagogue. She waves at the ushers at the door and I run around the car to open her door and help her up the steps. "You gonna wait for me here while I park?"

She shakes her head. "Nah, I'm going down front and talk with Helen. *She's* getting a new grand baby this fall."

I mutter under my breath as I help her up the last step, and hurry back to the car. I have to circle the block a few times before I find a parking space and I just make it inside as the doors are closing and the service begins. Bubbie pats the bench seat next to her and we spend a quiet hour following along with the service.

I say a quick prayer that just this once, we'll sneak out and immediately leave, but I know full well the morning has just begun. I used to take turns with my sister, Avi, driving Bubbie to services. My parents are somehow exempt from going except for the High Holidays...and to be fair, they do open the clinic on Saturdays to see newborns and their dazed parents.

But, Avi has moved to the suburbs. A few months ago, she got tired of the traffic crossing the river from the south and decided it was against the spirit of the sabbath for her to drive "all this way" to take Bubbie to shul. I close my eyes and listen to the choir and remind myself I like coming here. I like the stillness here, I like the predictability and cyclical nature of the service.

Autumn always means themes of forgiveness, renewal. Maybe this will be the year I feel renewed...

"Adriel!"

I whip my head to the side and realize my grandmother is shouting my name. She stands at the end of the bench with a pair of women, one old, one far too young for me. *Oh please don't let this turn into a setup attempt. Please, oh please, oh please.* "Yeah, Bubs? Sorry, I was...contemplating the readings."

Bubbie rolls her eyes. "Yeah right. Stand up, Adriel, and come see who I have here. You remember Ruthie Cohen? She's back from university. In Boston!"

The younger woman, Ruthie I guess, waves timidly. "Congratulations on graduating," I say, standing and making my way out of the seat. "Any job prospects?"

Ruthie opens her mouth to say something and her own grandmother butts in. "She's got offers from major banks all over the place. All over! But our Ruthie chose to come home here to Pittsburgh, didn't you, sweetheart? Gonna be working downtown."

Ruthie nods. I nod. "That's great," I say, tapping my fingers along the smooth wood of the bench back. I have nothing further to say to this 22-year-old my sister used to babysit.

Bubbie drapes an arm around my waist, pulling me close against her stout body. "Adriel is up for a major award. Science teacher of the year!"

I shake my head. "No, that's not it, Bubbie. I told you, it's a social dinner. Lots of teachers are invited."

She waves a hand and leans toward her friend. "They're giving him a cash prize."

"It's for the school, Bubs." I turn to face Ruthie and her grandmother. "The organization is donating funds to a few different public schools for STEM enrichment."

Ruthie's eyes go wide. "Are you a teacher? That's so wonderful. I bet your students love you."

I'm not sure what I've said or done to give her that impression, but I can objectively admit that the Franklin Middle School students do seem to admire me, so I thank her. I look over my shoulder. "Hey, Bubbie, things are thinning out here. You want to go grab coffee and I can get the car?"

She clucks her tongue again. "You'll come with me for that coffee, young man. And we'll stay for bagels, too." She turns to her friend. "Did they order them from the same place this time? I hear she trucks the water in from Manhattan so they taste just like a New York deli bagel."

I shuffle along as they argue the merits of various bagels.

My scientific opinion is that the minerals in the water from New York might contribute toward that perfect taste and texture of the bagels there. But I don't want to go off on a tangent about the chemistry of bagel production, so I just silently enjoy mine.

I appreciate that my grandmother wants me to be happy. I mean, really she wants me to get married and have babies because that's what Jewish culture says means she has succeeded as a grandmother. But ultimately, she'd like me to be happy. I can admit that I haven't been too thrilled with the world since Lara left me. I think again about Leo's suggestion that I see someone professionally about it.

By the time I dab my mouth with the napkin, finished with my bagel, I see that Ruthie has gone and my grandmother frowns at me slightly as she continues nibbling and chatting. Eventually I tell her I need to get home and prepare for my award speech, a small white lie that gets her to nod so I can trot off to grab the car and take her home.

There's always a chance I'll get called upon to say a few words at the dinner. My colleagues insisted I attend the science educator event, as head of my department. They know my background, and know that I know how to talk to rich people. They should also know I'm terrible at schmoozing, though I'd be lying if I didn't admit to feeling my heart race when I saw Samantha Vine is the keynote speaker.

Samantha Vine is everywhere I look these days, except when I draw up the nerve to try to speak with her at her own company. I wonder again whether Leo is right that she seemed interested. Or whether he's right that I need to get out there and just do something reckless and fun. She's busy with her company doing...whatever it is that's going on there.

I'm busy with my students and my empty apartment and my family.

I pull up out front of the synagogue and put my blinkers on, waiting for my grandmother to emerge. I decide to fire off a text to Samantha before I lose my nerve again. ***Saw your name on the science educators dinner. Hope we can catch up.***

Once I send the message, I stare at it in agony, worried it's the dullest message any man has ever sent a woman. I watch as it shows as "received" and I practically hyperventilate as the three dots appear on the screen. She's typing something back.

I wondered if you'd be there!

I wait, as three dots appear again, as if she has more to say, but then they stop. Nothing else. Her message conveys absolutely nothing about whether she, too, is interested in reckless fun of the naked variety. Frustrated, I shove my phone back in my pocket and drive my grandmother home.

CHAPTER FIFTEEN

Samantha

Shane pokes their head into my office, grinning. "I just got the cutest email," they say, walking to my desk with their iPad.

"You walked over here to show me? Why not just forward it to me?" I raise a brow and lean toward their screen.

"Because," they say, clicking open the window. "I want to watch your face while you watch it."

A video starts to play and I recognize the teens from Franklin Middle School who had come here for their field trip. Warmth spreads through my chest as I watch the shaky video panning the room of smiling, waving youngsters. "Yooooo, Ms. Vine! Our teachers said we should show you this stuff!" An unseen teen walks around a classroom, pausing at each desk where students are pecking away at their devices. "Since we all got these, Mr. T is letting us use your program to, like, write up our lab reports from this dissection." The screen zooms in on a girl whose face I remember, but whose name escapes me. The girl clicks her tweezers at me, beaming. The narrator flips his camera around and grins, braces glinting in the overhead light of the classroom. "This is actually pretty cool. So, yeah. Thank you!" He flips the camera again and he must count down from three, because all the students in the room yell, "Thank you!" And the video fades to black.

"Wasn't that delightful?" Shane bounces on their toes. "I wish we could use it for something."

I furrow my brow. "Why can't we?"

They roll their eyes at me. "They're minors, Sam. For all I know, the school didn't even authorize them sending us this video. It came from an email handle that included the word banging."

I laugh at that. "Sounds about right to me. Could you forward it to me, anyway? I promise to only use it for personal joy."

I pull up my phone to send a message to AJ about the video and I see that I never finished texting him about the science dinner. Ugh, he must think I was being weird. Fully expecting his voicemail, I call his number and gasp a little bit when he answers. "Why are you answering the phone?"

His voice is deep and unamused. "Did you call to test me or something? Isn't it normal for people to answer when the phone rings?"

"Well you never have before this!"

"I've never been available to talk when you called." He pauses. "Today I'm available."

"It's the middle of the day. Why are you talking on the phone while your students are sending me emails?" I have no idea why I'm getting snippy with him when I really do want to talk to him. Something just compels me to bicker whenever he opens his mouth.

AJ is silent for a moment and I hear him inhale before he says, "I'd like to pause and ask for clarification about the email. My students emailed you?"

I smile, unable to help myself. "They sent me the cutest thank you message. Well, they sent it to Shane, but they showed it to me. They're using Vinea to document their lab reports! And you're still dissecting frogs?"

He coughs. "We've moved on to sheep hearts. I hadn't realized they sent you something."

I frown. "You're not there with them? I guess that's why I don't hear anything in the background?"

"If you must know, I'm home sick today."

"Oh, I'm so sorry. I thought teachers never get sick? I remember some of my teachers telling me that they build these impenetrable immune systems. It inspired my science fair project one year in fact—"

"It's pinkeye," he blurts.

"It's what?"

"Pinkeye. Conjunctivitis. It's extremely contagious but I'm about to do my third treatment. Plus my Bubbie made me matzo ball soup, so I'll be back tomorrow."

"Wow, AJ. I haven't even thought about pinkeye for at least a decade."

He sighs again. "One minute I'm getting an all-faculty memo about it and the next, my eyes are crusty and itchy. I've learned my lesson about giving the students high fives."

"Aww," I squeal. "You give high fives! They love you. Seriously, I can tell." I hear him clear his throat uncomfortably. "Well, anyway, I just wanted to let you know I love the video and we obviously won't share it since we don't have releases from their parents or anything like that."

"I'd appreciate you sending it to me so I can see what they said."

"You'd have to give me your email address, Mr. Trachtenberg." Apparently I'm flirting with him now. Which, yes. I want to flirt with him. He's sexy, damnit. In a hairy, grouchy, untouchable sort of way.

"Surely you can get that information from Shane?" I can't read his tone, so I decide he's flirting right back.

"Or you could just tell me and I could send the video without interrupting Shane's work." He reads off his address. "Adriel? That's your first name?"

"It is, yes."

"But you go by AJ?"

"She says, as she goes by Sam." Okay that was definitely a flirty response.

"Fair. Okay, *Adriel,* I'll send you the super cute video your amazing students sent me. And I'll tell you it made my day. Things are rough over here."

Thank you, *Samantha,*" he parrots. A pause, and then, "The kids make my day brighter, too."

I smile and we're both silent for a few beats. "Okay, well, I guess I'll see you at the dinner thing."

"I'll be the one with the bloodshot eyes."

I must be sitting with a moony expression, because Audrey and Logan enter my office, take one look at me, and burst out laughing. "What in the world has you making that face?" Logan peers over my shoulder, but my phone screen has gone to sleep so she just takes a seat across from my desk and plunks her things on her lap.

I wave a hand. "Shane shared the thank you video the students sent after the field trip." I shrug. "It made me feel good."

Audrey bites her lip. "Well! I'm definitely glad you got some serotonin. Are you ready to review financials and then finalize your speech for the science educators dinner?"

I cringe. "Finalize?"

She blinks at me. "It's tomorrow, Sam. Let me see what you've got." Logan nods, encouragingly.

"I got a whole lot of nothing," I admit. "I was going to write it tonight." I cringe again. I was also going to sign off on the finance reports tonight. There's just not enough tonight to go around.

Audrey places her palms on my desk. "I know you know this, but you cannot continue to do everything personally." I slump a little lower in my seat, knowing she's right but also not sure how to rebound. Audrey rolls her eyes. "I'm going to send an emergency message to the agency we used for our last annual report. Maybe they have someone who can whip up some keynote bullet points for rush pay."

Audrey starts clicking away furiously on her laptop. Logan pops her lips a few times and decides to capitalize on the silence. "Moving right along to financials," she says. And for the next hour I listen intently as she and Audrey walk me through some of the basics I need to know before I speak with our board next week. It's going to be a long night.

CHAPTER SIXTEEN
AJ

From: Vinelli, Kellie
  Sent: Thursday, September 28
  To: [All Staff]
  Subj: Morning Middle School Memo!

Good Morning Faculty! Thank you to everyone who turned in progress reports! As a reminder, AJ Trachtenberg will represent Franklin Middle School at tonight's Science Educators Celebration and his student Margot Costa will give remarks! Attached you'll find some follow-up tips from Nurse Battle about staying vigilant during this latest outbreak of conjunctivitis!
  Have a great day On Purpose!
  Kellie Vinelli, Principal

I stand outside the robotics company hosting this dinner, wondering how in the hell anyone is supposed to recognize that this is a robotics company. I guess that's part of the intrigue of the whole thing. The brick building in the industrial Strip District neighborhood shows no outward signs that it contains state-of-the-art technology and boasts some of the top scientific minds in the industry on its payroll.

There's just a tiny sign beneath an awning. And, of course,

the swanky cars lining the street. I wonder if those belong to any of the other teachers attending or if they're all the deep-pocketed donors' vehicles. Either way, I remind myself, I'm about to eat fantastic food and celebrate some really cool opportunities for students.

I lean against the railing, waiting for Margot's arrival. She was beside herself when her essay was selected to be the highlighted student speech for the evening. I offered to give her and her mother a ride to the event, but as they declined, I decide to wait for them outside instead so we can all walk in together.

A few blocks away, I see a bus slide to a stop on Butler Street and they emerge, looking nervous. "Margot!" I cup my hands over my mouth to shout at them and then wave. I see palpable relief on her mother's face as they make their way toward me.

Margot's mother looks around, nervously. "Used to be, nobody would go to this neighborhood after dark," she says, biting her lip.

I laugh. "Ah, that was before the Pittsburgh Renaissance," I joke. This whole neighborhood used to be filled with Italian families who worked in the various factories that once lined Smallman Street. Ever since the new Children's Hospital was built here, there are fewer Moose Lodges and more craft breweries and, of course, hot new robotics laboratories in the renovated former factory spaces. "Seriously, though. I'm happy to drive you both home afterward so you don't have to take the bus!"

Margot grins. "I like the bus! I take notes for my sociology observations."

I nod, impressed. "You're taking sociology this year?"

"Mm hm. At the gifted program. I'm making notes about commuters."

I smile at her and then remember that I never learned her mother's first name. I stick my hand out for her to shake.

"You can call me AJ," I tell her, hoping she'll offer a response, but she shakes her head.

"Better to stick with the formalities. It'll help me feel better at this whole thing."

I redirect my attention to Margot. "Well, then, ladies. Shall we go inside?"

We step inside to another dimension. The lobby somehow feels naturally lit, even though there are very few windows in the brick facade. Soft classical music plays as we make our way down the polished concrete halls. A black-clad host offers to take our coats, but I didn't wear one over my suit jacket and Margot seems reluctant to part with hers. I wave a hand and try to get the Costas seated somewhere, preferably with some snacks.

The dinner is being held in a massive room, clearly an old assembly line area of the former factory, a space now flanked by offices. High-top tables decorate the perimeter and a stage has been constructed atop what looks like a giant funnel. "I wonder if that used to pour molten metal," Margot says, pointing.

"Don't point," her mother hisses, and I smile.

"I bet it did," I tell her. Finding our names on the seating chart, I glance around our table assignment, delighted to see we will be sitting with other folks from the city public schools. And then I see another name that stops me cold. As Margot drags her mother off toward the crudités, I stare at the seating chart.

I see Lara's name in neat, sans serif font, listed as the plus-one for the CEO of an autonomous vehicle company headquartered here in the Strip. Lara is here with the folks footing the bill and I'm here with the kids receiving the financial support. I feel nauseated. I feel enraged that my ex is going to be here on the arm of her new, wealthy lover. And here I am, still the lowly science teacher in a poor, urban middle school. And then on top of it all, I feel shame for feeling this way. Of course my students depend on these contributions from local businesses. I chose this work, helping students envision a different and more prosperous future. My boss won't come out and say it, but my upbringing makes it possible for me to be a liaison here.

I look over at Margot again and shake my head. I'm not going to allow myself to forget why I do this. Margot can't change the circumstances of her beginnings, and neither can any of her classmates. But I can help her and all these students change the trajectory of their future. That's why I do this. That's why my whole family lives a life of service. We care about people, damn it.

I make my way to the bar and grab a bottle of lite beer, chugging down half of it as I mentally prepare myself to see Lara. I'm sure she'll look good.

But then I look up to see Samantha Vine gliding into the room and I can't believe I ever thought Lara looked beautiful. Samantha is sunshine and radiance. Everyone around her knows her, or pretends to, anyway. An entourage of people follow her as she makes her way to the front table, setting her wrap over the back of a chair. I watch as she greets people and kisses cheeks.

I watch as Margot makes her way toward Samantha, too, and I clench my jaw, waiting for a cold dismissal. But it doesn't come. Samantha squeals in delight upon seeing Margot and throws her arms around my student. I watch as she enthusiastically shakes hands with Margot's mother and then seems to introduce them to the people standing all around her.

I'm so intent on watching them that I forget to look for Lara. So of course I'm caught off guard when I hear her voice. "Is that really you, AJ? What on earth are you doing *here* of all places?"

CHAPTER SEVENTEEN
AJ

I turn, beer still held to my mouth, and I swallow. "Lara," I say coolly. I don't feel the need to remind her that I'm a science teacher or that this is a celebration of science educators, so I just stand, expectantly, as she clings to the arm of her date, a man in skinny jeans and Converse sneakers. At a formal dinner.

The guy looks between Lara and me and makes a face. He eventually sticks a hand out. "Lance Dallas," he says. "I'm here with Voyager."

I return his shake, hoping my hand is cold and wet from clutching the beer. "AJ Trachtenberg," I tell him. "I'm here with Public Schools of Pittsburgh."

His eyebrows shoot up. "For real? Wow, man. That's noble of you."

"That's me," I clench my jaw again. "Noble." I watch Lara's hand as she traces Lance's pec, and I note the glistening skating rink on her left ring finger. She sees me see it and I don't miss the look in her eyes. A smug expression that conveys *see? I found myself a real man with real ambition who buys me real jewels I deserve.*

I'm spared from continued small talk with my ex when someone clinks a spoon against a glass and asks us all to find our way to our seats. "Guess I'll have to catch up with you later," I say, but I don't look at either of them as I shoulder

86

my way to my seat. Margot is bouncing in her chair when I arrive.

I try to rein in my foul mood, but it's difficult. I keep looking across the room at Lance and Lara, even when I know I'd rather be looking across the room at Samantha Vine. Why do I always seem to choose the path that punishes myself?

"Mr. T did you see Ms. Vine is here? And she remembered me from the field trip!"

"Well I'd hope she'd remember you. It was just the other day."

She sighs. "Yeah, but there were like 100 of us. She knew my *name.*"

Margot's mother beams. "Your name is on the program, too, toots."

"That's true! Mr. T, did you see?" She waves a program in my face so I can see her name typed on the order of speakers, right after Samantha Vine's remarks. It occurs to me that, as title sponsor of the event, Samantha's company has given more money to the cause than Lara's fiancé gave. I don't like how that makes me feel smug. I look back at Margot's name, reminding myself to stay focused on my students. The light in my life. Everything else is just a fruitless distraction.

"They spelled it right and everything," I say, plucking a roll from the basket in the middle of the table. I give a wave to my colleagues from neighboring schools and we chat as the wait staff passes out the salad course. Once everyone is chewing, Samantha makes her way to the stage.

I'm supposed to focus on her words, I'm sure, but I can't get past the sight of her in a dark green wrap dress. It nips in at her waist and flares out, stopping right below her knees. The neckline isn't scandalous by any means, but the way it hugs her chest makes my pants feel uncomfortably tight in the crotch. I adjust my tie as she begins speaking and I find myself jealous of the microphone that gets to be pressed so close to her ruby red lips.

This whole experience is like a sine wave for me. I vacillate between rage and distracting lust. Leo is definitely right, I decide. I need to jump this woman's bones. Or…ask her if she's interested in that. I don't even know how, but my body needs me to try. Nevermind the fact that every time I speak to Samantha, we wind up snipping at each other. She doesn't need to consider me as relationship material. Everyone needs a good time once in awhile. I could give Samantha Vine a good time.

I listen as she talks about what an honor it is for Vinea to fund summer learning opportunities for children as well as professional development for educators. I'd be lying if I pretended not to be excited about the summer workshops in chemistry and biology. Eventually Samantha calls Margot up to the makeshift stage and leads the applause. Samantha stands off to the side, listening attentively. Margot talks about opportunities like the field trip Vinea sponsored and mentions a summer coding camp she's evidently earned a scholarship to attend.

The room laughs at Margot's self-deprecating poverty jokes and applauds at the poignant moments. And then I stop listening because I watch Samantha pull a cell phone from a pocket in her dress and stare at the screen instead of listening to Margot. I practically growl as Samantha backs off the stage, making her way out of the room while Margot continues speaking, unawares.

I can't believe she's running out while my student is talking. The very same student she greeted so warmly a few minutes ago. How rude can one woman get? I look up and catch Lara glaring at me as I glare at Samantha. I drag a hand through my hair, realizing I'm falling apart. I have too much baggage to successfully attend these sorts of community events for our school. Why in the hell does Principal Kellie Vinelli keep choosing me for her exclamation-point-peppered ideas? I feel like I can't escape the lifestyle Lara was so desperate to pursue.

My chicken dish is served and I find I can't even taste it above the depths of my outrage. Margot returns to the table, beaming, unaware that her new hero so rudely ignored her while she was speaking. That just infuriates me further. Once I congratulate Margot on her poise and excellent speech, I excuse myself from the table and prowl off in search of Samantha.

I have absolutely no idea what I'm going to say or do when I find her, but I hear her voice coming from a room off to the side. Following the sound of her shouting, I make my way along the dimly lit hall.

From the sound of Samantha's muffled voice, she's pissed about being asked to drive someone somewhere. Figures. She probably has a driver. I'm sure Lara and Lance have a driver. They probably all have butlers.

I'm so busy stewing in frustration...okay, maybe a speck of jealousy...that I shout when the office door suddenly flies open and Samantha bursts halfway out of the room. My shout startles a server carrying a tray of desserts as she passes me in the hall.

There's a shriek and a crash behind me. Samantha gasps. I turn to see a tray of plated cake slices toppling to the floor as the server moans. "No," she wails. "No, no, no not again!" She drops the tray she'd been carrying and covers her face with her hands.

Well shit.

I can't have this woman losing her job over my nosy outburst.

"I'm terrible sorry," I say. "This was entirely my fault. Please let me speak with your manager to tell them so."

The woman shakes her head and sighs. "I'll just dump all the cake in the trash barrel. This sort of crowd doesn't ever eat it anyway. Maybe my boss won't even notice."

"NO!" Samantha and I shout it at the same time, startling

us both. Samantha squeaks and I look over to find her still standing there, her face contorted in horror. "Did you say you're going to throw this away?" Samantha stoops and begins picking up some of the plates of cake. She balances a few of them on her forearm like she's been slinging plates in a diner her entire life. This woman is constantly shattering my expectations. Or something.

The server looks at Samantha strangely and starts trying to take the cake away from her. "Ma'am, this has been on the floor. Of course it has to be thrown away."

"Oh, come now," I say, putting on my best teacher voice. "Half of these landed plate-down. Nothing touched the ground." I start picking up small plates, too, grateful the thick acrylic plates didn't shatter under the decadent dessert. The cake slices are beautifully presented. Dark chocolate sponge with a fudgey icing and a raspberry sauce decorating the plates.

"We can't just waste them," Samantha says, and I find myself nodding in agreement with her. A moment later, the caterer backs away from us with half the floor-cake, muttering under her breath about "crazy-ass rich people."

I look at the plate in my hand and realize she's talking about me, both the absurd part and the presumed wealth. I guess I really do look good in this suit.

Samantha remains crouched next to me, working to stand without upsetting the balance of cake plates in her arms. She's not being careful about the drape of her skirt, and I catch a glimpse of black lace between her thighs as she wobbles on her heels before finally making it back up to her feet.

She bites her lip and looks over her shoulder. "We can't just waste these," she repeats.

I'm breathing heavily now as I, too, stand up. "We definitely cannot." She looks over her shoulder at me as I enter the doorway. Samantha starts stacking plates of cake on a desk in the office, and blushes when she sees how I'm watching her. I can't help it. Between her reluctance to waste good dessert and the way she looks in that damn dress, I'm struggling to keep myself together. Samantha brushes past me, en route to gathering another armload of cake. Her breath hitches as she watches me stoop to pick up more plates. When I walk into the office to set them down, I see she's begun digging in to one of the pieces of cake. She pauses to lick icing off her knuckle, and the sight is so hot that I finally lose my   fucking   mind.

CHAPTER EIGHTEEN

Samantha

AJ Trachtenberg has me pressed against a desk, and his erection is digging into my stomach. My hand hovers in the air near my mouth as I stare into his dark eyes, flashing in the light of the office whose door he just kicked shut on his way to pounce on me.

His chest heaves as he takes my face in his big, hairy hands and before I can finish licking the frosting off my lips, he's doing it for me. His tongue is hot and wet and I groan at the feel of it parting my lips.

I draw a shaky breath as I feel him moan into my mouth. I lean in to the pressure of his palms against my cheeks, melting back against the desk as he kisses the hell out of me. And then abruptly stops.

"What?" I hiss at him, leaning forward in an attempt to grab his tie and pull him back against my mouth.

"I'm furious with you." He clenches his jaw and I see a vein bulging in his neck, right where his dark hair curls a little bit behind his ear.

"You're always furious with me." I reach for him again and he wraps his arms around me, pulling me up from the desk, against that delicious body of his. He's so tall and firm and fuck! I wonder if the rest of him is as hairy as these beautiful hands now splayed across my ass.

AJ buries his teeth into my neck and it hurts so good. I lean into him, thrusting my hips against his, desperate for some sort of friction. He backs away again.

"You made me make that poor woman spill cake," he growls. And then he sticks two fingers into a slice of cake on one of the plates and I watch, transfixed, as he picks up a glob of cake and brings it to his mouth, his pink tongue coming out to lick those beautiful digits clean.

"I made you? What? I was taking a phone call from my father about his eye surgery." I should put my hands on my hips or tell him to mind his own business, but I don't. I just reach for a plate and start feeding myself some of the cake AJ dug into with his bare hands.

I start to wonder if the cake tastes like AJ. Or if AJ tastes like cake. I glare at him around my index finger, licking icing off my nail.

His face shifts, slightly. "I didn't know your father was sick."

I stab a finger into the cake. "He's not fucking sick. And he can take a fucking cab to get his cataracts sliced off if my brother isn't available. I'm not. Flying. There. For. This." I stab the cake with each word and finally scoop a giant mouthful of cake toward my face.

I feel a clump of it fall onto my chest as I cram the cake into my mouth and I groan around the mouthful. "Dis is so gut."

AJ has stepped closer to me again, his nostrils flaring a bit as he breathes, staring at me while I chew. He reaches out and wipes his finger along my collar bone. Slowly. So slowly. I feel the rasp of his calloused skin against my chest and my breath catches while I wait for whatever he has planned next. As I swallow the cake, AJ dips his head and licks my skin.

I'm done. I've melted and I'm done now. I start to sink and, feeling me topple, AJ picks me up and props my bottom against the edge of the desk. He uses his hand to brush the plates of cake to the side to make space for me and then he steps in between my legs.

Wow. Just wow. Why on earth have I not been seeking out party sex with grouchy, bearded, hairy men? As I catch my breath, I decide I want more of what I just had. I want more of the cake, more of the kissing, more of this sexy shoving his body against mine, please and thank you.

"You drive me wild." He's leaning over me like I'm a barbell he's about to heft up, his hands splayed on the desk beside my skirt. I look at his crotch and I actually see the fabric of his pants twitch as his bulge throbs in there. I reach for it, cupping him, savoring the way his head falls forward like he's on the brink of passing out.

"I've always been wild," I tell him. I hear the music pick up outside and figure the speaking portion of the evening must have ended. People are probably looking for us. I can't find it in me to care. I've been so stressed out, so busy, so frantic. And right now, I've got decadent buttercream and hairy man and all of it is mine to eat. For right now.

I start to unzip his fly, but AJ catches my hand. "We don't even like each other. This isn't right."

I arch a brow at him. "Who said anything about liking each other? I don't need to like you for you to fuck me on this desk."

His eyes flash. "Is that what you want, Samantha?" I like the sound of my name in his mouth, the way his plump lips look as they press together to pronounce the M. The way his tongue peeks between his teeth on the TH sound. I'm so close to him I can see it all, and rather than answer him, I grab his tie again and pull him against my lips.

But wait. No. I'm not supposed to be doing this here. He's mad at me for some reason, and I'm mad at my family and this is a benefit event for science educators. I need to go be responsible and … he pulls back from the kiss and takes a few steps away from me. "What are you doing?"

AJ shakes his head rapidly and begins adjusting his tie. "AJ." I cross my arms over my chest protectively, feeling exposed and chilled in the absence of his body heat. "What are you doing?"

I watch him swallow and lick his lips, lips I know taste like cake. "Samantha, I…" He runs a hand through his hair and sighs. "I need to get back out to Margot and my colleagues. I shouldn't have followed you or eavesdropped on your call."

"I don't care about that," I spit out. "Why did you stop—touching me?"

Rather than answer, AJ gives his suit a final pat and grabs two plates of cake from the desk. Without another word, he balances both plates in one hand, opens the door, and leaves the office. "Huh," I say out loud. "So this is what this feels like." I have never had a man initiate sex and then walk away before either of us reaches the crescendo. I do not like this.

There's no way I can go back out there and just mingle with people. I have icing residue on my chest and I can still feel the echoes of AJ's heat tingling along my front. I eat a piece of the cake, trying to decide what to do, and notice the fire safety map posted by the door to the office. Studying it as I dig into another slice, I see that I can circumnavigate the party and sneak out the front by way of the coat check.

I grab a slice of cake for the road and get the hell out of there. By the time I reach my car, I realize my tears have gathered and are now leaking from the corners of my eyes. I touch my cheek in surprise. I don't typically cry. Who has time to sit and feel feelings? "Oh boy," I mutter, shoving a final bite of cake in my mouth and tipping the plate into a trash can as I dig my phone out of my pocket.

I need to talk to someone. I bite my lip. My friend Orla has a baby and I don't want to wake her up with a call. Esther is probably elbow deep in bar patrons and I'm pretty sure Logan was looking forward to a night on top of her Callum. I press a knuckle into one of my temples, fretting. I've been working so hard lately. I really, really could have used a pleasant, sexy diversion tonight.

Instead I'm maybe crying a little bit in the dark, alone. I need a mom right now. Isn't that what people would do when something like this happens? Call their mom and vent about the awful man who rejected their advances?

Orla also lost her mom. She'd know what to say right now. But she's also been telling us all about how Nora is teething and not sleeping. "Shit," I mutter, unlocking my car and sinking inside.

"Are you cursing at me?" I hear a voice coming out of my phone. "Hello?"

My eyes widen and I fumble for the screen. "Oh, god, Orla, I must have boob-dialed you or something. Were you asleep?"

She yawns loudly. "I was not asleep, actually. I'm driving to the freaking north hills to get eye drops for the rabbit. Did you know rabbits can get pinkeye?"

"I'm sorry. What are you talking about?" Suddenly I forget why I was so upset as Orla vents the details of her husband's pet rabbit's conjunctivitis. She tells me about playing Rock Paper Scissors with Walt to see who "got" to leave the house to get the eye drops while the other adult stayed home to manage baby bedtime.

"This is so weird. AJ had pinkeye the other day!"

"The grumpy science guy?"

"Yeah."

"You know that shit is super contagious, right?"

I had not considered that. I tap at my face, wondering if I got pinkeye from making out and didn't even get an orgasm out of it. "Can I just skip to the part where I called you cursing?

"Yes," she says. "Sorry. Distract me with tales of a world that doesn't involve massaging a small mammal's tear ducts."

I shake away the mental image Orla paints and remember

the tears. "AJ fucking Trachtenberg," I mutter. I tell her about the floor cake and the sexy kissing.

"Sounds promising," Orla says. "Why are you calling me cursing instead of going for round two?"

I groan. "There wasn't even a round one. He just...stopped."

"Come again?"

"I'd like to come the first freaking time! Orla, he just stopped. Licked my damn collar bone, sucked the frosting off his finger, and smoothed his tie and left the room."

She makes a humming sound. "He sure does send some mixed messages."

"Thank you! It's weird, right? Does he think I'm gross? Is he kissing me on purpose to mess with my head?"

"Listen, I'm about to arrive at the vet hospital, but I think it's safe to assume he's not purposefully messing with your head. From what you've said he seems very starchy."

"Starchy is a pretty good adjective here, yes."

I hear the click of her turn signal. "I wonder if it scared him to give in to his passion like that? Sam, I see the vet tech waving at me. Let's talk through this some more after I deal with the rabbit eye."

I sigh. "It'll simmer. I'll probably just go home and fall asleep."

She laughs. "I've met you, Samantha Vine. You will go home and agonize over this and then do something amazing with your frantic worried energy, like build an algorithm to catalogue men's facial expressions or something."

"That's not the worst idea you've ever had..."

She laughs again and we hang up. I feel slightly more validated hearing Orla agree that AJ sent confusing signals, but try as I might, I can't let go of the sting at having him walk away. I don't run to my computer to build out an algorithm as Orla suggested, but I do spend most of the night combing through resumes from Shane and Audrey, sorting them into piles and hoping I can trust my team about hiring more staff. Clearly I can't trust my own instincts these days.

CHAPTER NINETEEN

AJ

Leo agrees to meet up for breakfast at the bakery near school. Provided I buy, of course. My hands are still shaking as I approach him, seated at the little cafe table on the sidewalk. I can't even pretend it's because I had too much sugar last night.

Leo taps his chin and then crosses his arms over his chest as I sit down. "You look like shit, Trachtenberg."

I nod. "I've been eating my feelings. I think I understand what that means now."

He arches a dark brow at me. "You're going to have to elaborate. You just used the F-word with me, man."

I puff out my cheeks as a server stops to take our orders. I roll my eyes as Leo orders a week's worth of pastries in a to-go box. "Well," I start again. "Lara was there last night."

"Oh, shit!" He beckons for the server to come back and orders an entire pot of coffee for us. "Was this the first you saw her since...everything?"

I nod and tell him about her ring, her smug expression and my snowballing emotions, ending with me leaving Samantha alone on the desk with all that cake.

"You left her there? Just licked and left?"

I close my eyes and nod. When I open my eyes, he's got his phone out, tapping away furiously. "Who are you texting?

This is private, Leo."

He talks with his mouth full. "I have to at least get Doug's take on this, man. This is advanced. This is honors-level friend work and I'm more of a remedial pal."

I shake my head rapidly. "No, Leo, please. You're not remedial. You've been such a good friend and I just want to forget that this ever—"

"Oh, good." Leo drops his phone back into his jacket pocket. "Doug is on his way. Oh, wait, yep! There he is. He did say he was close. Doug!" Leo waves his arms as our colleague parks across the street and then drags a chair over from the next table. It's early enough that we're the only people seated outside.

"I hear my services as a married man are required?" Doug grabs a pastry from the box and Leo nudges the coffee pot closer to him as Doug opens his travel mug to fill up.

"I have no explanation for walking away from Samantha Vine last night," I moan. "Hell, I have no explanation for kissing her in the first place."

Doug laughs. "No explanation? Come on, AJ."

I stare between them, waiting for one of them to offer some sort of advice. Something to make me feel human again instead of this quivering ball of...what have I become, exactly? When neither of them says anything, I admit, "She's intoxicating."

Leo nods. "And you're into her, man. You find her attractive."

"Yes, obviously. So what do I do about it?"

Leo shakes his head and Doug groans. Leo leans forward and slaps the side of my head, causing me to yelp.

Doug says, "AJ, I've been married for a long time. I'm married to a very loud, very assertive woman. I'm here to tell you to be straight with this woman." I wait for him to continue.

This is evidently the wrong response because Leo smacks

me again. "Call her," he says. "Tell her you're an idiot and you want to apologize to her."

"In person," Doug adds. Leo nods.

What they're suggesting sounds so logical, and yet more difficult than I think I can manage right now. "I don't think I can call her. I humiliated her."

Leo takes a long sip of his coffee and sets the white mug down gentle on the metal table. "I know you don't want to hear this right now, but all of this shit about Lara? How she made you feel like you're trash? You need to work on that."

"Work on that? I'm working on trying to forget her, actually."

He shakes his head. "You still believe all that shit she said, deep down. That's why you walked away from Samantha last night and that's why you're hesitating about calling her. Because you don't think you're worth her time."

I feel my guts churn as his words hit a little too close to home. I swallow as Doug pats my hand. "I agree with that assessment. And if you were one of my writing students wrestling with imposter syndrome, I'd assign you some mantras." He nods and leans over to his shoulder bag, pulling out a pad of sticky notes and a pen. He quickly scribbles "I'm an awesome person" on one of the notes, peels it off, and tries to stick it to my sweater. It falls into my lap.

Leo moves to pick it up and I swat his hand away. Doug says, "It'll stick better to your mirror. That wool you've got on is something else. But really, AJ. You're a catch. She's a catch." He shrugs. "Just call her."

I look at the note, trying to decide if he's right, if I'm letting my baggage from Lara interfere with … everything. Leo gestures for Doug's pen and writes in scratchy handwriting "I'm a dead sexy, hairy wolf." I laugh and feel a little better, which I suppose was the entire goal of calling Leo this morning.

"I still don't feel like I can just call, though. I need, like, a warm-up gesture to smooth things over." I take a nibble of a scone and watch Leo's face transform into a wide grin.

"Send her some cake, man." He points at the bakery. Doug holds out a hand for a high five, which Leo offers with a resounding smack.

"Cake," Doug grins. "Who doesn't like cake?"

Leo snickers. "We've already established that both AJ and Samantha are fans of the medium." Doug checks his watch and they gather up their stuff to leave. "See you in a bit, man."

I brush off the table and open the door to the bakery, hearing the bell tinkle as the door shuts behind me. The woman working behind the counter smiles, recognizing me from outside. "Get ya anything else?"

I stick my hands in my pockets and wince. "I need a good apology   cake."

CHAPTER TWENTY

Samantha

Invasive Vine? Pittsburgh Tech Startup CEO Too Flighty for Lasting Fame
  Isaiah Childers, Forbes correspondent

"There is no bottom." I stand by Audrey's desk and take off my shoes. My mom used to do that when she got home from work—take off her high heels and drop them inside the front door and just dive in to whatever disaster awaited her, whether that was peed sheets to wash or the frenzied clutter from getting three kids out the door for daycare in the morning.

Audrey raises a brow at me when I set the shoes next to her desk. "You okay? Wait. I can see that you're not. Let me start again." She looks up to Logan and Shane, who are cringing around a print copy of *Forbes* magazine. Audrey stands up and places her hands on my shoulders. "We love you. And we're a team here at Vinea. And we're going to figure out a solution to this."

The feature story about me has run in today's edition, and the reporter did not paint a flattering picture. Shane looks particularly irate as they stare at the magazine. "I hate this part where douche canoe calls you flighty and distracted," they say. "If you were a man, this would probably be a glowing analysis of you managing multiple irons in multiple fires." Audrey snorts.

Logan bites her lip. "This doesn't seem to have been edited very well," she says. "There are no quotes from your major early investors. No interviews with anyone from the board. It's like he wrote a day in the life piece but only captured the stressful parts of your day!"

I take a deep breath and squat down to pick up one of the shoes. And then I bang the heel of it on the polished concrete floor a few times while roaring in frustration. The heel snaps off the shoe and Shane gently plucks the ruined footwear from my hand, shaking their head. "Sam, let's be solution-focused."

They look up at Logan, who takes a deep breath and sits down on the floor next to me. Shane and Audrey follow suit, just sitting on the floor in their fancy work clothes while I noisily fall apart. I might be able to handle an article slamming me on a normal day, but not after getting rejected and not when we're on the cusp of bombing our IPO. I look at Logan, hoping she will come through with some good news in the face of this very public shaming.

She pats her thighs. "Okay, so most important is we've got growth and profits out the wazoo. From a numbers perspective, we are golden." She raises her brows and nods at Audrey. Audrey raises her brows and claps her hands.

I shake my head. "This article was supposed to prop me up as the leadership beacon the company needs to forge ahead. Our board is going to want…I don't even know." I start rubbing my temples.

Shane pats my shoulder with the hand that is not holding the shoe. "The board will want to know you've put wheels in motion to hire additional leadership talent. Check!" They hold up the shoe to outline a checkmark in the air. "We fast tracked the candidate for the marketing, which is great timing!" Their voice gets a singsong quality as they gesture with the shoe. "The new person was between jobs after having a baby and can start immediately. I'll just text them that immediately can be today."

My spine crushes in on itself a little as I consider that the solution to this problem is out of my personal control. The answer to Vinea's new public relations crisis is to winnow more and more administration of the business out of my hands. "Doesn't this make me a big failure?"

Logan looks confused. "What would give you that idea?"

I gesture all around me. "I am a disaster at the helm. I'm steering this ship into an iceberg. And other captain metaphors..."

Logan pats my arm. "Can you list any major companies where one person does all the work?" I blink at her a few times. She continues with her leading questions. "Do you have secret advanced degrees in business administration or strategic development?" I shake my head and she smiles. "Sam, honey, this will always be your company. You will always be the founder and it will always have your name on the building." Logan shrugs. "You just get to partner with more people now to keep the momentum."

Logically, what she's saying registers. But on the heels of dinner with my father, and conversations with my family, and AJ's rejection...all I hear is that my failure to woo that *Forbes* reporter is costing me the opportunity to bring Vinea to the next level. "When's our next board meeting? I need to go to my office and prepare."

Shane shakes their head. "Sam," they say. "Let's on-board the marketing pro and get their take. We hired someone to shape board remarks. Let's use that expertise."

I snap my eyes to each of my team's faces. "Okay, so what do you suggest I do? Go sit in my office and work on my cuticles?" They all cross their arms and squint at me. I wince. "I'm sorry for my tone. What should I do?"

My fingers itch to go code something, to find a solvable

problem and dig in. Audrey's face brightens and she pulls up an app on her tablet to show me. "First of all, I'm renaming myself Operations Manager or Chief of Staff," she says. I gesture for her to continue. "We're working on the policies and procedures piece of the IPO packet and you've got a binder of codes of conduct, employee handbooks, and workplace hygiene documents to read carefully and sign off on."

I wrinkle my nose. Shane slides me a business card. "You've also got one more conversation with a potential board member and I think you'll really like this one," they say.

I look around at them and back to the *Forbes* article sitting up on Audrey's desk. She reaches up and flicks the magazine into the recycling bin. "Okay," I tell them. I nod. "Okay. It's good to have a to-do list."

"Yes," Logan says. "Love a good list." She squeezes my leg and the three of them hustle off toward the kitchen. I realize we've had this intense conversation before most of the staff even arrives. My stomach grumbles, but I ignore it, heading to my office to bury myself in paperwork.

A few hours later, my desk phone rings and when I answer, I don't recognize the voice on the other end. "Ms. Vine?"

"Yes?"

"I'm Noelle? Audrey hired me as admin?"

"Oh. That sounds nice." I move to hang up the phone but Noelle continues.

"We've had a delivery for you. Would you like me to bring it in? It's just that there's a Do Not Disturb sign on your door…"

Did I put that up? I honestly can't remember. My stomach growls again. I'm not taking good care of myself today. "Yes, Noelle, please bring in whatever it is."

A perky brunette enters my office carrying a bakery box.

My interest is piqued. "Here you go, Ms. Vine." She sets the box on my desk and tucks her hair behind her ears, like she's waiting for me to open the package.

"Call me Sam," I mutter as I run a nail along the seal on the pink box. I lift the lid to discover a thick slice of decadent cake. I gasp. My stomach growls loudly and my mouth waters.

Noelle peers over my shoulder. "Oh that looks yummy," she says. "There's a card inside!" She points along the back of the box, where a lined index card is wedged behind the cake.

To my knowledge, this has not been on the floor. Regards.
—AJ

I stare at the note, uncertain what to make of his words. I flip the card over, but there is nothing else. No further note on the back. Noelle squints as she reads over my shoulder. "That's a weird note, Sam," she says. She puts her hands on her hips. "You want me to get you a fork?"

"Please." She hustles out of the room and I stare at the tidy, slanted handwriting. What am I supposed to make of this? On the one hand, the man went out and bought me cake. And either had it delivered or brought it to me at work. But this note…is he flirting?

Noelle returns with the fork and I inhale the first half of the cake, pausing to savor as I move on to the rest of it. I check the time and realize it's late enough in the day that AJ is probably done teaching. One more bite of cake and I pull out my phone to send him a message.

What's with the note?

He writes back almost immediately. *You got the delivery?*

I send him a selfie of me with a forkful of cake.

He calls me. I answer but neither of us speaks. I huff. "This is all really weird, Trachtenberg. Seriously. What's with the note?"

He groans. "I was trying to be flirty. You know. Floor

cake. The party…"

"This is you flirting?"

He huffs. "Yeah, well, we can't all be good with people. You're welcome for the cake." My phone beeps as he hangs up.

"What the fuck? What the actual fuck?" I call him back. "Are you trying to get under my skin? Are you in cahoots with the *Forbes* people?"

"Who? No. Oy vey, Samantha. I'm trying to get into your pants." I pull the phone away from my ear and stare at it. When he speaks, it sounds like his voice is tiny and far away. "God, I am colossally terrible at this. Objectively bad. I'm sorry. Forget I called. Forget I sent you weird notes and cake."

"No!" I shout at him as I bring the phone back to my ear. "I will not forget the cake, sir. This cake is excellent. Where's it from? There's no branding on the box."

"I'll tell you if you tell me where Vinea gets its coffee." I can hear a laugh on the edge of his words. I like it.

"If I knew that answer, I'd give it to you. Audrey used to handle the coffee but she promoted herself so I'm not sure what happens next."

He blows out a breath. "Can we start over?"

I shake my head. "No. I don't want to start over." I grip the edge of my desk and decide to just say what's on my mind. "I want to pick up where we left off."

"What does that mean to you exactly…"

"The part after you were licking frosting off my collar bone but   before   you   ran   out   of   the   room!"

CHAPTER TWENTY-ONE

AJ

I did do those things. I licked frosting off her peachy smooth collar bone and fled the scene in terror when I realized how much I like her, how much power that gives her to hurt me. "Well," I respond. "Did you save any frosting? For licking purposes?"

"Are we actually going to do this or are you going to leave me with blue ovaries again?"

"Blue ovaries?"

She snorts. "Men get blue balls. I want an equivalent thing for when a man gets me all lathered up and then sneaks away."

I close my eyes and swallow. "I vow to leave you fully satisfied if you give me another opportunity."

"I'll text you my address." She hangs up the phone and I stare at it as a message comes through with her info.

I'm not sure how long I stare at the phone before Leo and Doug strut into my classroom. Doug actually has a bag of popcorn and Leo raises a brow at me. "Did you take care of it?"

I nod. "She…sort of commanded me to come to her house later. Is that normal?"

Doug nods while Leo shakes his head. "Nothing about this is normal, hombre."

Doug talks around a mouthful of popcorn. "Just bring her something, man. Flowers or chocolate." He shrugs. "Amy always appreciates a frozen margarita."

I look at my watch. "You think I should show up at her house with alcohol?" Both Leo and Doug nod. I sigh. "I'm going to mess this up again. I should just cancel. Send her some apology beer."

"No," Doug and Leo shout at the same time. Doug hands Leo the popcorn and clasps my shoulders. "AJ. Adriel. Do not cancel. Stop and grab a bottle of Prosecco. Take it to her at her house. Go."

I nod and stand up, grabbing my bag stuffed with all the papers and tests I need to grade this weekend. Obviously, I wasn't able to concentrate enough to do so last night. Leo pulls a tin of mints from his pockets and opens it. I grab two and crunch them. I swallow and leave my friends. In my mania, I neglect to stop at the liquor store and as I stand on Samantha's stoop I debate running away again to go get the booze.

Before I can complete that set of mental gymnastics, the door flies inward and I'm being hauled inside by my tie.

"Let's get one thing straight," Samantha says, tugging my tie for emphasis as she kicks her door shut. My eyes widen. "You are absolutely not leaving here until I come. Last night was just plain rude and it's not fair to leave a woman in that sort of state."

She releases my tie and I stare at her. "I apologize," I mutter. "I fully intend to—well I can do better. By you. In terms of orgasms."

Samantha rolls her eyes. "Is this you groveling?" Her annoyance triggers whatever force last night allowed me to manhandle her in that office.

"You're always swinging that big tech energy at me," I growl, backing her into her living room. I spot a couch over her shoulder and steer us toward it until her ass hits the back of the leather upholstery.

She stares at my crotch and licks her lips and only then do I begin to pay attention to how fucking hard I am for her. My dick is throbbing inside my pants. I can practically feel the scratch of the zipper through my boxer briefs and I move a hand to open my fly, just to relieve the pressure.

Samantha likes this. I can tell by the way her breathing increases…and also because she bunches up her skirt and spreads her legs wide. "God, AJ, yes. I need you to fuck me with that thing."

I have my dick in my hand now, giving myself slow tugs as I stare at her, watch her practically beg me to invade her. How long has it been since I found relief from anyone other than my own hand? I groan as she lifts her skirt.

She adjusts her hips, spreading her legs more so I can stand between them. "You were fucking teasing me in that hallway," I grit out, my fingertip stroking her upper thighs. I skirt the area of her panties, never touching them. Teasing as her breath increases.

"I did no such thing," she pants. She digs her fingers into my shoulders, waiting.

"Mmm hmm, you did." I skate the pad of my finger along the seam of her panties and she moans. I feel a surge of heat and wetness and my cock jerks in response. "Your skirt fell open while you squatted on the floor, picking up cake." I drag my fingers near her clit while I talk and she leans back, her spine curving like a comma. "Admit it, tease." I bend over her, my mouth close to her ear.

"I wanted you to look at me," she whimpers, and as soon as she says so, I slide a finger inside her panties. "Holy shit," she moans. She clamps around my finger and groans as I press a thumb against her clit. She is all softness and scalding heat as she begins to writhe beneath my touch. I love how it feels to make her feel good.

"Ooooohhh, god. How are you so good at this?"

"You like that?" I arch a brow, a little surprised that my fingers can bring her this much pleasure.

Samantha grabs my cheeks in both palms. "You better keep doing what you're doing, Trachtenberg."

I grin. Her eyes glitter in the afternoon sunlight and the next thing I know she's kissing me. I respond thrust for thrust, my tongue matching the rhythm of my finger as I stroke her until the dam bursts.

Samantha bucks her hips and nearly falls over the couch. I feel like an orchid, my limbs wrapped around her awkwardly as I try to hold us both up and keep from hitting the ground as she comes all over my hand.

"Fuck, that's hot," I hiss, nibbling at her collar bone as she comes. I already feel better about damn near everything.

Samantha's pupils are huge, her movements languid as I slide my hand out of her body. Her mouth hangs open and she smiles. "AJ Trachtenberg," she slurs. "Sex expert." Still half slumped over the couch, Samantha runs her hands along my chest.

My hands fumble in my pants pockets, seeking my wallet and the lone condom that only lives in there because the school nurse handed them out to all the faculty at a training. I say a quick prayer that whatever brand the public schools purchased in bulk is effective and I roll the condom on as Samantha yanks my tie again.

She grabs the wrapper from my hand and throws it, and then her hand is on my cock, guiding it toward her wet heat. I think I black out from the pleasure as she shoves me inside her. I grip her shoulders and thrust. I feel the bare mound of her pussy against my pubic hair and I grunt like a caveman, rutting against her without withdrawing.

She loves the friction of that move. I feel the flutter of her muscles gripping me tighter, and so I continue hammering against her. I'm ramming her against the edge of the couch now, probably bruising her ass cheeks, but I'm beyond caring. "I didn't know it would feel this good," I groan.

Samantha starts moaning and biting whatever she can get her teeth on. She bites my ear and my nose before she clamps down on my tongue and I yelp in pain. Startled, I pull out and stare at her. "I don't think so." Overcome with a surge of emotion, I spin her around and pin her hands down to the frame of the couch with mine. "Keep them there," I say, using one of my hands to line myself back up as I toss her skirts up with the other. I slam into her from behind, staring at her ass jiggling with the force of my intrusion.

This sex is hot and dirty and totally unlike me, and I don't even care because it feels so damned good. Samantha shakes her head, tossing her blonde hair. I feel the silken strands of it brush against my arm and I gather it up in one hand, lazily tugging on it as I fuck her. She moans. "You like that?" I tug harder and she groans, louder this time. "Sshhh," I hiss against her ear. I lean over her, putting my full weight on her back as she's bent over the sofa.

Sam keeps moaning louder, so I cover her mouth with my palm, half worrying she'll bite my hand, half hoping she'll leave a mark. I feel her breath against me, coming in short bursts, and then she starts thrusting her hips back to meet mine as I ram into her faster and faster. I hear the sounds of our bodies slapping together in the living room, and I smell her arousal mixed with the latex and my own pre-cum. It's a buffet of senses and as I feel her white teeth sink into my calloused hand, I know I'm nearly gone.

I reach around Samantha's hip and find her clit again, burying my fingers in her folds and swirling in the rhythm that drove her mad the last time. I press my lips to the place where her shoulder meets her neck as I press my thumb into her clit and together, we topple over the edge of bliss. "I can feel you," she pants. "I feel you filling me up inside."

I'm spurting like mad, mildly concerned I'll overflow the condom with pent up desire. And then I'm drowning in the aftermath of bliss. My senses dull and I practically fall asleep, still inside her, still half hard. I feel her ribs expanding beneath me as Samantha draws deep breaths, also trying to recover.

Eventually, I slide my hands from her mouth and hip, letting my fingertips graze her ass one last time. I commit the sight to memory, the round globes of her backside as my wet cock slides out of her body.

Sam turns around, using her forearm to brush her hair back from her face. What we just did felt powerful, a surge of relief mixed with a heady danger. Emotionally, I cannot afford trysts with beautiful, wealthy women. Not anymore. But she looks sated and perfect and I know without a doubt that she has the power to destroy me. I pull off the condom as I stare at her, terrified.

She bites her lip and looks at me, concerned, and asks, "Am   I   going   to   get   pinkeye?"

CHAPTER TWENTY-TWO

Samantha

"What?" He blinks at me. Just stands there with a wet condom in his hand, his pants sliding down his legs, blinking.

"You said you had pinkeye and my friend Orla says it's really contagious and, well, your hands have been all over me...am I going to get pinkeye?"

AJ laughs, and the sound shatters the tension and worry I had been building in the moments since he pulled out. I'm not exactly sure how I went from blissed out to worried about contagion so quickly, but here I am. Half naked, disheveled, concerned.

"I don't think you're going to get pinkeye, Samantha." He looks around, probably in search of a trash can for the condom, and I push off the back of the couch, nodding for him to follow me to the kitchen.

"How can you be sure?" I shimmy my undies back into place and smooth out my skirt a little, waiting my turn to wash my hands at the sink. It feels...nice, standing next to him in the kitchen, talking about eye germs, washing hands together.

AJ turns to me, grabbing a dish towel to dry his hands. I stare at those fingers again. I love his hands, I realize, not just for how they made my body feel but for the shape of them. Long and elegant, calloused and sturdy, all at once. His voice is smooth and reassuring as he says, "I told you, I did a course of the eye drops. Look—I don't have any lingering redness." He opens his eyes wide, which makes me giggle.

"True. No bloodshot residue." He hands me the towel and I dry my own hands before looping it back over the handle to the oven. I turn to face him, crossing my arms over my chest. "You're not going to leave, are you?"

"Do you want me to leave?" He arches a dark brow and I shake my head.

"No, AJ. Adriel. I want you to stay. I probably want you to bang me again later. After we eat something."

He grins. "Glad we cleared that up." He looks around the kitchen. "I guess this is your place?"

I smack the counter. "Ha! I should give you a tour, right? Offer you a drink? I'm doing everything backwards." I gesture around the kitchen. "This is a room I never use, except for the fridge and microwave. You're familiar with the sofa. There's a powder room and laundry back there." I point toward the little alcove behind him.

My townhouse is small but it has everything I need: tiny deck, tiny yard with a tiny tree. I pay someone to deal with plants out there so it generally looks nice.

"This isn't what I was expecting," AJ says, peering out the sliding glass door to the patio.

I notice a heap of negative press articles I was torturing myself by reading and quickly gather those up and flip them over. "You thought I'd live in a sleek condo or something?"

He shrugs as he pulls the door open. I hear cicadas and feel a rush of warm air. The light is orange and I realize we might be about to experience a sunset together. Or something. "I thought you'd live in a penthouse," he says, stepping outside and leaning on the deck rail. I follow him out and stand next to him.

"Are you disappointed?"

He shakes his head, looks at me for a moment, and then

drapes an arm over my shoulders before gazing at the horizon again. "This house suits you," he says. I'm surprised to realize I'm glad he approves of where I live. I'm further surprised to feel myself leaning in against his shoulder, resting my cheek against his wool sweater and feeling his body heat as the sky quickly shifts to brilliant purples and pinks.

We lean on the railing as the city slides into twilight and whatever spark there was between us...it doesn't melt away with the light. It morphs into something different. Something, frankly, a little bit scary for me. I like leaning here in the stillness with Adriel Trachtenberg. I liked the furious coupling in my entryway, sure. But I like this quiet with him, too.

I place a hand on the rail and he moves his other hand close to mine, tapping my pinky with his. I grin at him. "We could walk up to Mad Mex," I tell him. "Get some margaritas and giant burritos..."

AJ loosens his tie and undoes the top few buttons of his shirt, giving me a delicious peek of chest hair above the collar of his sweater. He picks up my hand and kisses my knuckles. "Or," he says, and licks the dip between my index and middle finger, "we could order it for delivery and you could show me your bedroom while we wait."

I feel a rush of heat through my center at his words and I raise my eyebrows. "You have some really good ideas," I tell him.

He nods. "Did you save any of the cake?"

I spit out a laugh. "Please! I inhaled that as soon as I got it."

He shrugs and tugs my hand, heading back inside. "I assume those stairs lead to your room?"

"Aren't we going to order the food first?" I trot along behind him, nearly tripping over the shoes he toes off in my kitchen. He's in a real hurry here.

"I'm too distracted." AJ squeezes my side, causing me to yelp as his touch tickles. He steps behind me on the stairs, lifting my skirt as I walk up toward my room. By the time I've led him to the door, he's pulled my blouse over my head and unfastened my bra, and a sigh escapes my lips when he spins me in his arms. "I want you very badly," he says, easing the strap off my arms and tossing my bra to the side, leaving me naked apart from my panties. "In case that wasn't clear earlier."

I swallow. "I want you, too. A lot." He nods and lifts his sweater and shirt off together, revealing the hairiest chest I think I've ever seen. I gasp and dig my fingers into his fuzz. "Oh my god, I love this," I coo. "It's like a pelt."

"A pelt? Seriously?"

I nuzzle my cheek against his pec and lick the pebbled nipple peeking through the dark hair. "Yes. A pelt. I love it." My skin seems to glow in contrast to AJ's. I begin tugging at his belt but he lifts me up and sort of hurls me at the bed, both of us landing on the mattress with a grunt.

"I wish I had more frosting to lick off you," he says, exploring one nipple and then the other as I continue reaching for his zipper.

"Well, we already played that game." I cheer as I manage to unfasten his pants and he hisses when I find his cock inside, hard and hot like the last time. And then he jumps off the bed and I sit up, confused. "What are you doing?"

He's bent over, wriggling out of his pants as he picks up his tie from the tangled clothes on the floor. "Another game," he says, tugging the tie between his hands. He pauses. "Blindfold or tied up?"

My jaw drops. "I want to see you," is all I can manage before he nods and climbs back onto the bed, grinning as he crawls between my legs and lifts my arms above my head.

"Good," he says. "I like this idea better anyway." He loops the tie through the side of the headboard and pauses as he knots it around my wrists. "I've never done this before," he admits. My breasts are lifted in this position and I feel exposed. I really, really like it.

"Me neither," I confess, wriggling to get comfortable as AJ considers his work. He nods, smiles, and then bends his head to bite my breast. I moan as he plays with my nipples, tickles his fingers along my sides. Tied up like this, I can't reach out and dig into his hair or stroke that thick cock of his. I'm just lying here, enjoying myself. And AJ makes it very, very enjoyable. Nobody has ever done this—created a scenario where all that's expected of me is to enjoy myself. I want to whimper at the very idea of it.

He pauses periodically to smile up at me as he kisses my lower belly, strokes my thighs, and presses my legs wider. I groan as he licks between my legs, feeling his shaggy hair tickle my stomach in contrast to the warm, wet pressure of his tongue on my clit. "Oh shit, that feels good," I moan, straining against the tie. My back bows up off the bed as AJ licks and strokes.

"You're delicious," he purrs, giving me another lick before sitting up on his heels, one hand on his cock, the other toying with my wet folds. "Tell me you've got condoms up here?"

I nod. "Drawer," is all I can spit out, hoping it's true, that I still have some in there and that they're not expired. AJ leans to the side and flicks on the bedside lamp, filling the room with a warm glow as he rummages in the drawer. He holds up my vibrator, nodding at it, and then finds the box of condoms, making a delighted sound as he extracts one foil packet.

I lick my lips, watching as he rolls it on. I expect him to slide inside me then, but he sits beside me, touching me and toying with my clit, driving me insane. "What are you doing?" I pant, lifting my hips up toward him, growing desperate.

"I believe this is called edging, Samantha." He emphasizes the M and Th sounds again, like he did the first night.

"Ooh, you're terrible," I groan, but I know what he's doing now. He's building me up, dragging me right to the cusp, and then backing off. And each time I can tell that whatever is building is bigger and more powerful than anything I've experienced to date.

Finally, when I can't take it anymore and I'm glistening with sweat, tugging against the tie, he stretches out over my body, lines himself up, and slams inside me. Both of us cry out. One of my hands slips free of the tie and I drop it to his back, feeling him move. Lying this way, his hips dig into my pelvis just right and my head drops back onto the mattress as I feel a crescendo building in my spine.

"Oh, god, I'm so close. So close, so close," I pant. AJ wipes my hair back from my brow and presses deep inside me. He stares into my eyes as I shatter, spasming around him and straining on the tie, digging my fingers into his shoulder.

"Samantha," he whispers, rolling his hips along with mine as I come and come and come. "Samantha," he says again before his body stiffens and he roars. I feel him pulsing inside me and I gasp as the final tremors of both our climaxes threaten to shake the room apart.

CHAPTER TWENTY-THREE

AJ

I wake up in a pile of nacho chip crumbs and blonde hair, trying to find the source of the ringing noise that yanked me from an amazing dream. Gradually, I realize it wasn't a dream. I'm still naked, still tangled in bed with Samantha Vine and the remnants of our late-night "funky fresh Cal Mex" feast.

The pieces fall together. We shared to-go margaritas. We started eating burritos downstairs and finished eating chips and guac upstairs, with enough sex in between that my dick feels a little chapped. And now it's Saturday. Saturday.

"Shit!"

I sit up, whipping my head around the room in search of my phone as Samantha rolls onto her side and makes a groaning sound. "Wazzamatter?"

"I'm so late. I have to take my Bubbie to the synagogue." I find my phone and silence the alarm, trying to decide what to do. I simply don't have time to go home and shower. Stooping to gather up my clothes from the floor, I nearly trip over Samantha, who is inexplicably standing in my way.

"What's a bubbee?"

I blow out a breath and wince, worried I just hit her with some foul post-burrito halitosis. "My grandmother. I take her to our synagogue every week and I have to pick her up in…"

I look at my phone screen. "Ten minutes. Shit, shit, shit."

Samantha nods. "I'll come with you. Grandmas love me."

I freeze. "Sam. You can't come with me. Come on." I start hopping into yesterday's pants. My clothes are wrinkled but still presentable. This can be okay. I glance up and she's glaring at me, nostrils twitching.

"You don't want me to meet your Bubbie? After I bought you burritos?"

I make a sound between a hiss and a moan, fumbling with the buttons on my shirt, staring incredulously as Samantha quickly steps into some sort of one-piece flowy pantsuit. Is she even wearing a bra? "Samantha, I really don't have time to discuss this right now." I glance around the room, patting down my sweater and blowing a breath into my palm. This is a nightmare.

She shakes her hair and looks ready for the limelight. Seriously, how is this woman so effortlessly gorgeous? She makes a wicked face at me. "I'll lend you a toothbrush if you take me with you."

Five minutes later we're both crammed into my Fit. I still have no idea what's happening here but I have no time to contemplate the impact of showing up to shul with a woman. Bubbie is going to interrogate me for hours about this. Hours. As I pull up in front of her apartment, I decide it's not actually such a terrible thing if Bubbie and the other yentas jump to conclusions about me and Samantha Vine. I look at her again. She's smearing some shiny gloss on her lips, wearing mirrored sunglasses that match her outfit. She's a knockout.

Compared to her, I look exactly like what I am: a wrinkled grouch. But actually, I'm not really all that grouchy today. Apart from the chapped penis, I'm feeling pretty good. And then my grandmother screams.

I didn't even notice her coming out of her building, but as

she peers into the window of my car, noticing Samantha, Bubbie shrieks and clutches her chest. Panicked, I scramble out of the car and run to her side. "Oh my god, Bubbie! What's wrong?"

Samantha eases out of the car, her face etched with concern. "Mrs. Trachtenberg? Are you all right?"

Bubbie grips Samantha's arm, her hand like a claw as she stares into Sam's face. "Adriel," she whispers. "Who is this gorgeous creature?" Samantha beams, seemingly relieved that my grandmother is just being dramatic, rather than having a stroke.

"I'm Samantha Vine," she says, patting my grandmother's hand. "I'm the reason your grandson was late this morning. He told me how important punctuality is to you, and I just wanted to apologize in person." My grandmother looks like she's going to faint in a puddle of bliss.

"Adriel," she croaks. "You are forgiven. But you are in so much trouble for keeping this vivacious woman a secret. Is she coming to services? Tell me she's coming with us to services. Rose Ackerman is going to explode when she sees."

As if the matter is settled, my grandmother reaches for the back door of the car and makes to hoist herself inside. Samantha gasps. "Mrs. Trachtenberg, no! I insist you sit up front with AJ. Let me climb there in the back." And again, as if the matter is settled, Samantha ducks into the back and clicks her seatbelt into place.

My grandmother beams as she climbs into the car. She twists herself around to face Samantha, utterly ignoring me, and asks, "How do you know my Adriel?"

Samantha peeks over the top of her sunglasses. "It all started with a big misunderstanding," she says. "But then we mended fences at an event this week."

Bubbie claps her hands. "The teacher of the year awards! Are you a teacher, too? Isn't it wonderful how Adriel was being recognized?"

"Bubs, I told you, that's not what it was."

Samantha chuckles. "He was being recognized, though. And his student, Margot, was a speaker at the dinner. She sent me her talk afterward. That gal is going places!"

I meet Sam's eye in the rearview mirror. "Margot sent you something?"

She nods. "Yes, I got her mother's information from the program organizers. Margot's already going to the coding camp this summer but I made sure to let her mother know how vital those sorts of public speaking skills can be, even in the realm of computer science."

"Samantha owns a tech company," I tell my grandmother as I pull up in front of the temple.

I wait for Bubbie to climb out but she just glares at me. "I'm not going in there alone and miss the chance to see everyone notice your new girlfriend, Adriel. Go ahead and find a parking place and we'll all walk together."

"Oh, I'm not sure about...girlfriend isn't...I..." Samantha looks panicked as I drive slowly up the street in search of a parking space.

"This is all very new, Bubs," I tell her.

My grandmother snorts. When I finally park the car, she climbs out and clings to Samantha like, well, like a vine. I pop my emergency kippah on my head and smile, watching the two of them mount the steps to the temple. Every person within earshot listens as Bubbie introduces, "My AJ's Samantha, isn't she gorgeous?" And I like the sound of that, the implication of her as mine. I keep waiting for Sam to reveal something, some discomfort at the association with me, but it doesn't come.

She shakes hands with all Bubbie's friends and laughs at their jokes and seems to genuinely enjoy the butterscotch candies they offer as we find our seats. In the years we were together, Lara only ever reluctantly joined my family at services on the major holidays. And even then, she pouted the entire time like she had somewhere better to be.

Samantha just invited herself along this morning even after I told her she couldn't come, and honestly I'm not sure what to make of it all. But I do know that I'm sitting in shul with my arm around Samantha Vine, like we're a couple. Like I'm someone she cares about in return. As she snuggles closer to my side, I allow myself to believe it.

CHAPTER TWENTY-FOUR

Samantha

I have no idea what the hell I'm doing.

I mean, I know what I'm doing. I'm inserting myself into AJ's family life like some clingy girlfriend. I just don't understand why.

The thought of him brushing me off again, even to go take his grandma to church—wait. I can't say *church* for Jewish people. Synagogue. Why in the hell did I invite myself to the synagogue with him? Am I supposed to talk about hell with Jewish people?

"Samantha?" AJ nudges me with his shoulder.

"Hm?" I smile at him and realize the service has ended. He gestures toward the aisle and I gather my things hurriedly, rushing to stand next to his smiling grandmother. As soon as he's on his feet, he startles me by pressing a kiss to my cheek. A casual, light touch of his lips, as if he's used to doing that. As if this is something we do together—kiss for no reason. I flush, delighted by the attention. And then my racing thoughts take charge again, wondering how on earth I came to be here.

A man's family and religious outings shouldn't be part of whatever I needed to sort out in my head. I just wanted AJ to stop being mad at me. Didn't I?

Well, I also wanted him to make up for leaving me hot and bothered at the science educators dinner. And he made up for that. Repeatedly. I didn't even think I'd want him to sleep over after all that, but we got to eating burritos in bed, and talking about true crime documentaries…and here we are. Unshowered, wrinkled, at temple with his Bubbie.

"And this is *Samantha*," Bubbie says, emphasizing my name like I'm the most important person she's ever met. I smile at the perky older woman who has approached us in the aisle.

"Pleased to meet you." I shake her hand as I feel AJ stiffen at my side. He draws his arm around me possessively and when I look up at him, his face has regained some of that cranky crust I'm used to.

Bubbie pats my shoulder. "Samantha owns a business! Isn't that something? Samantha, this is Nancy Cohen. My Avi used to babysit her Ruthie."

I can't quite make sense of who Avi and Ruthie are, but I smile warmly regardless. Nancy furrows her brow. "Is your family from here, Samantha? I don't recognize you."

"Oh, I'm a military brat," I say, really hoping to steer conversation away from my family. "I grew up all over."

"Samantha is the founder of Vinea," AJ says, his voice steady and perhaps containing a note of pride. "Her company has been very good to my students."

I grin at him. "I'm glad to finally hear you admit that! Your students are amazing, by the way. It's a good thing you threw a temper tantrum and made me call you to apologize."

He guffaws as Bubbie looks at him strangely. AJ says, "If only you just called! Bubs, she stormed into my classroom. Unannounced."

Mrs. Trachtenberg gasps. "Oh, Adriel does not like to have his lesson plans disrupted." She shakes her head and I laugh.

"I gathered that much." I slide my arm around his waist and squeeze. "But it worked out in the end."

I shiver as I feel AJ's fingers running through my hair, gently, and again somehow possessively. Like he's claiming me through the motion. We walk to another room in the building, where there are tables heaped with bagels and coffee.

I beeline for the coffee as I feel AJ's fingers reaching to clasp mine. He's really leaning in to acting like a boyfriend here, and I don't hate it. I give his hand a squeeze as I wait my turn for the coffee. A teenager pours me a mug full and I add a splash of milk, take a sip, and purse my lips.

I look at AJ and he nods. "It's burnt, shitty coffee, Samantha. This is what people drink outside of your world."

"My world?" I arch a brow at him and try to decide what to do with the coffee. Exhaustion wins out and I take another reluctant sip.

"Your world," he repeats. "Vinea, where you somehow manage to have the best coffee I have ever tasted in my entire life." He takes the mug from my hands and places it on a folding table and then takes both my hands in his, meeting my eyes. "I'm begging you to tell me your source. This is me." He squeezes my hands for good measure. "Begging."

I laugh. "What will you give me for this information?"

He turns his head slightly and frowns, but his eyes twinkle and I know we are still flirting. And I'm still enjoying it. "Almost anything you want," he whispers, just as his grandmother sidles up to us again.

She squeezes my arm. "Samantha, I don't know why my Adriel waited so long to tell me about you, but I want you to know I am so glad to meet you. You have to come join us this week for brisket."

"Well, I'll try my best to clear my schedule if you send me the details."

Bubbie smiles and sighs. "It's so good to see you happy, Adriel." She leans toward me conspiratorially. "He's been a mess since that business with Lara. Terrible thing, how she left him."

AJ swallows. "Bubs, please let's talk about something

else."

She shakes her head. "Honestly, who does she think she is? The Queen of Sheba? Anyway, he's found you now and I can already tell I like you better." Bubbie pats my cheek, and when I look at AJ he's clenching his jaw, his entire body stiff and his demeanor has grown dark. I smile, but feel uncomfortable in the tension. When AJ says he's ready to head out, I feel relief.

As we drive her home, Bubbie talks about the meal she and her children will be preparing for me…sometime in the future. "What can I bring? This sounds delightful." I lean forward in AJ's tiny car to better hear his grandmother, but AJ screeches into a parking spot outside of her building.

"Samantha has a very busy schedule, Bubbie. Let's make sure she's actually free before you assign her part of the meal."

I open my mouth to protest, to say I meant it when I'd clear my schedule, but he glares at me in the rear view mirror. I snap my mouth shut, confused. As Bubbie exits the car and waves, I just barely manage to get myself in the front seat and buckled before he peels out, aiming the car toward my house.

"What's up, AJ? You're acting strange."

He's silent as he shifts gears and checks his mirrors for pedestrians before turning right. I smile, enjoying how carefully he drives, how he actually shares the road. "You're the one who said you're swamped preparing for your company going public."

He accelerates to try and make a yellow light, which turns red, and he slams on the breaks, growling. I grip the handle above the window. "I can make time to eat a meal. What's this really about?"

He looks over at me. "Two days ago we were barely speaking to one another and now you're joining my family for holiday meals? You don't think that's a little inappropriate?"

I swallow, recoiling from the sting of his words. "I like you, AJ. Why are you being hurtful right now? You got weird when your grandmother brought up your ex."

He grunts. "Well, my ex makes me feel really fucking weird, Samantha."

My eyes widen. "Okay, well, maybe sort out your feelings about that before you come back to my house for another booty call."

He turns into my driveway, stops the car, and runs his hands through his hair. He takes a few deep breaths and then turns to face me. "You're right. I'm sorry I got moody."

I hesitate as I loop my fingers through the latch to open the door. "So am I invited for brisket or not?" AJ's face shifts around, like he's experimenting with different moods and expressions. I roll my eyes. "Just forget it." I pull the door open and start to climb out of his tiny car.

He places his hand on my arm when I reach for my purse. "What if we tried a date first? Just the two of us? Without my parents…"

"A date?"

He sighs. "Yes. I'd like to ask you out. If you're still interested."

"What sort of date?"

AJ pauses, as if he can tell that his answer will determine whether I tell him to fuck off forever or invite him back into my bed. He licks his lip and says, "Would you like to help me document chimney swift migration patterns?"

I gasp. Data? Science? Birds? "Yes." I nod. "Very much yes. Text me the info." I close the car door and wave as I head back inside my house. In a single morning, AJ Trachtenberg has managed to tug me through most of the major emotion groups. I'm going to go back to bed while I'm riding the current "fellow geek sees my passions" high.

CHAPTER TWENTY-FIVE

AJ

"She came to church with you and your grandmother?" Leo and Doug stare at me in the teachers' lounge as they share a bag of baby carrots.

I nod my head. "I mean, we call it a synagogue. But yeah." I tell them about Samantha inserting herself into my morning and how nice it felt. How I could almost allow myself to believe that this could be a regular thing. Not a one-off. Not some weird fluke where she got in a mood. I was the one in a mood... "She seemed eager to meet Bubbie for some reason."

Doug shakes his head. "Not 'some reason,' man. She's into you."

I wince. Leo munches a carrot, nodding. "She's definitely into you. I think it was the apology cake that sealed the deal."

I reach for the bag of veggies, considering. "Do I really want to woo a woman who is actually turned on by my fumbling attempts at romance? I told you what I ended up writing on the cake note, right?"

"There's a fish in the sea for everyone," Leo says. "Or something like that." The bell rings and Doug rolls up the carrot bag, sticking it back in the fridge. He and Leo grab their worksheets from the table by the printer, leaving me alone in the lounge. This is my prep period, but I'm not making notes about our upcoming unit on birds, or how they differ from reptiles.

No, I'm sitting alone in a room, staring out the window and thinking about how nice it felt to hang out with Samantha Vine this weekend.

Until Bubbie brought up Lara. Just hearing her name curdled my stomach, made me remember all the vows I made to myself about not risking that humiliation again. No more wealthy women, I swore. Or women who desired that sort of status. So what do I go and do? I start falling for a woman with a literal billion dollars of investment, whose name is all over the press and whose company swings Big Tech Energy.

I chuckle, remembering Samantha using that phrase. She's always witty and self-deprictating. I try to remind myself what Leo has insisted all along, that Lara is an idiot asshole. *Her words say more about her than me*, I repeat. But it's really fucking hard to change the thought patterns that have been etched into my life the past few years.

After school, I rush home to change into jeans and hiking boots before swinging by to grab Samantha for our birding date. I still can't believe she's into this idea. I'm mainly checking it out to see if it's a good citizen science opportunity for my students. The local Audubon society hosts these events where people try to count the chimney swifts, keep track of how frequently the visit their familiar haunts. It hadn't actually occurred to me that Samantha's software would be perfect for this sort of project, especially the way it lets people share data.

I pull up to her house and nearly faint when she pops out her front door wearing tight jeans and a fitted flannel shirt. This woman has the body of a Baroque sculpture, with thighs I long to squeeze again.

Samantha opens the door to my car and climbs in, grinning. "I brought binoculars," she says, shaking a small, expensive pair. "I wasn't sure what all we'd need."

"Just our eyes and something to take notes," I say, still

staring at her. My car is filled with her scent, her shampoo and her soap. It's distracting.

"Notes?" She arches a brow. "You know what I do for a living, right?"

I nod. "I'd love to see how we can take field notes using Vinea."

She smiles, a broad, bright expression that fills my car with light. I can't go another second without kissing her, and so I do. I lean forward and wrap my hand around the back of her neck, pulling her close, and just kissing her. She moans softly, happily, resting her hand on my shoulder as she returns the kiss. "Hi," I say when I pull back. She tucks her hair behind her ears and buckles her seatbelt. I grin and begin driving as she fiddles with the radio, clapping her hands when she finds the local public radio station, which is playing bluegrass.

"This seems like excellent birding music," she says. "Although, I guess we need to be quiet while we're watching?"

I nod. "But we don't need to be quiet on the way there." She taps her thighs along to the music and chats with me about the stress of her work day. She apparently intends to dive back into paperwork when I drop her off this evening. It's just about dusk when we arrive at the park where we're going to sit and observe the chimney swift tower, a tall wooden structure built by Audubon volunteers to attract the birds so they don't try to nest in people's active chimneys.

Samantha seems delighted as I grab a blanket and snacks from the hatch of my car. "I didn't know you were going to feed me," she says, settling next to me on the ground a safe distance from the tower. "How does this work?"

I shrug. "We just wait," I tell her, offering her some crackers and pre-sliced cheese, which she takes, her hand lingering against mine.

"Aren't you missing a meal with your family?" She

whispers, which isn't entirely necessary but I like how it necessitates us sitting closer together, so I don't say anything about her volume.

"Nature calls," I whisper back. "Or something like that." We wait in comfortable silence for awhile and, seeing no birds, Samantha asks for more details about the project. I explain how the organization raised funds to build these towers throughout the area. "Hundreds of birds might roost in each one during migration, like right now, but the birds are extremely territorial. So only one pair will nest in each tower during nesting season."

"So you brought me here to look at grouchy birds who like to be alone?" She nudges me with her shoulder.

"Not alone," I respond. "With their mate. And their babies. But nobody else."

"That actually sounds pretty nice," she says wistfully, looking at the skyline again, pulling up her binoculars and frowning when she doesn't see any birds. "Oh!" She exclaims and then slaps a hand over her mouth. "Are those the birds?" She whispers and points and sure enough, a dozen or so chimney swifts swoop and loop from above the trees, making their way toward the tower as the sky rapidly darkens.

"It smells like rain," Samantha says, not taking her eyes off the birds.

"Petrichor," I say, trying to count how many I see.

I lose my place when Samantha says, "Petri what?"

I start to count again, pointing with my finger. I note two dozen birds and then turn to her. "Petrichor. It's the word for how it smells when it's going to rain."

"There's an actual word for that?"

I nod, reaching for her. I drape my arm around her as we watch the birds tumble through the air. She gasps as they swirl, forming a funnel cloud, then a spiral, and then finally dive into the wooden tower just as the skies open up and rain begins to fall in the rapidly growing darkness.

But she doesn't run toward the car. She brushes her wet hair back from her face and cuddles against me, mesmerized, until the last bird sinks into the roost. "Thank you, AJ. This is amazing." Her lips are warm against mine as she turns in my arms in the autumn rain. We kiss until the world fades away, until I forget that we're in a county park in a populated urban area. Until she presses gently on my shoulders and I lean back on the blanket, pulling her on top of me, and feeling her settle between my legs.

"Wait," I say, clasping her hand. She looks around.

The park is deserted between the dusk and the rain. Samantha grins and shakes her head. "I don't want to wait," she says, sliding a wet hand down the waist of my jeans. I groan, feeling her fingers reaching for my stiffening cock. When she wraps her palm around my shaft I gasp. It feels so good to be touched, to be wanted this way.

"I don't have anything," I stutter around her kisses. "Condom I mean." Samantha doesn't stop stroking me but rolls to the side, resting her elbow on the blanket.

"Then we won't have intercourse," she says and, with a damp rush, she tugs my jeans open and sinks her beautiful mouth to meet my sensitive skin. If someone had suggested that I, AJ Trachtenberg, would be getting a blow job in the rain in the park, I...well I wouldn't have laughed because I don't do that very often. But I certainly wouldn't have thought that was realistic.

And yet, here I am, gasping and moaning as my hands stroke Samantha's golden hair, watching as her lips slide along my cock, dying of the pleasure of it. Of the forbidden nature of oral sex in nature.

"Fuck, Samantha, fuuuuuuck." She holds me steady with one fist as the other traces along my stomach. She alternates firm sucks with long licks of her tongue. She swirls around my tip and my hips jerk up in response.

"Mmm," she sighs as she works. "I've wondered what you

taste like."

"You have? Oh shit. Oh shit oh shit oh shit."

"Mm hm." She pops off the end of my dick, drooling a little in a way that should be disturbing but is instead deeply arousing. "You like this?"

"Oh, god, Samantha, yes. Yes, shit. I'm going—I'm so close. So close." My entire body stiffens as I feel my orgasm building in my spine, overtaking my entire nervous system. Samantha lowers her mouth even further and I feel my tip slide along the back of her throat before I erupt into her mouth. I pant and gasp, shuddering as she swallows, stroking my thighs and my stomach as the waves of pleasure ebb.

"That was really hot, AJ,"she says. When I arch a brow in confusion, she laughs, leaning on her elbow on the blanket beside me as I lie in the rain with my junk exposed. "I like making you fall apart," she says. And damn it, I like it when she   makes   me   fall   apart,   too.

CHAPTER TWENTY-SIX
Samantha

Eventually AJ and I climb back into his car and blast the heat. He lets me wrap the blanket around myself as the dark settles in and the air gets a lot colder, quickly. The rain stops as we drive back to my house. "The petrichor smell is getting stronger," I say, biting my lip as he pulls up outside my house.

I want to invite him in. I don't have time to invite him in. But I want to invite him in. He smiles in the glow of the streetlight. "Soon it'll just be miserable when it rains. There's nothing more dreary than rain in November."

"But rain in autumn is fine?"

He nods. "Petrichor," he repeats, reaching out and touching my face. There doesn't seem to be any purpose to his touch, other than a desire to feel my body.

"Come inside?" It comes out as a plea and I feel myself clenching, desperately hoping he doesn't turn me down.

He smiles and nods, turning off the car. I climb out and look at the damp blanket I had wrapped around me. "I could put our things in the dryer," I tell him.

"Then I'd have to stay for the whole cycle," he says, leaning on the wall next to my door. "Don't you have to work tonight?"

"I can spare an hour," I tell him. I hand him the blanket and unlock the door. He follows me inside and I stoop to unlace my sneakers. He does the same and then follows me up the steps to the laundry, where I toss the blanket into the dyer. "Want me to dry your…shirt?" AJ grins and strips off his shirt, standing in my laundry room topless and hairy.

I feel suddenly bashful, and I grab a robe, tossing it on as I drop my damp clothes into the dryer. This is all really unexpected, both the vulnerability and my desire to have him stay but not fuck me right now. He just leans on the dryer, grinning, like he's perfectly content to stand in my laundry room half dressed while I'm in a robe. I clear my throat. "Will you tell me about your ideal tool for recording the bird migration observations?"

He arches a brow and tilts his head, like the question took him by surprise. "Ideal tool? I guess." I head down the stairs toward my living room, where my laptop is nestled on the coffee table amidst a heap of my homework from Audrey and Shane and Logan. AJ follows and plunks onto the couch, reaching for the blanket I have draped over the back. He wraps it around his shoulders and then drapes it over both my knees when I sit next to him.

He runs his fingers through my hair. "We need to track the date, number of birds observed, a space for behaviors…oh and the number on the tower."

"There was a number on it?"

He nods. "There was."

I sigh, leaning a little more deeply into him. "Okay, well what are you hoping to note with all these observations?" As he lists out info about migration patters and population health I realize it's like a lullaby for me. Never in my life have I snuggled on a couch with a man as he talked data and correlation to me. "God, this is nice," I blurt out, and then touch my fingers to my lips. I hadn't intended to say that out loud.

But AJ nuzzles closer and presses a kiss to my temple.

"This *is* nice." His voice is a gentle, low lullaby. I reach for my laptop and pull up the Vinea web-based program. With a few clicks, I've got a simple bird observation tool set up, and with a few clicks more, I've got it labeled for Public Schools of Pittsburgh with AJ as the project administrator.

"There," I say, gesturing at the screen. "Your students can make bird notes and share them. Or not share them. But based on your project goals, it seems like you'd want to share them with other birders, right?"

He stares at the screen for a long time, and without saying a word, he pulls the laptop from my hands and sets it gently on the table. "What are you—" He pivots on the couch so he's facing me, his body twisted around mine. He cups my cheek with one hand and leans in, kissing me so gently, so slowly and deeply.

A sigh escapes my lips as his tongue explores my mouth. He pulls back and looks into my eyes, his thumb caressing my cheek. "I love that you did this for my kids," he says, letting the blanket drop from his shoulders.

"It's nothing," I breathe. "It's what my software already does."

"It's everything," he says, and then he slithers down to the floor, on his knees on the area rug as he peels open my robe. "I want to thank you properly."

"You don't have to do that." My words are punctuated with gasps as I feel his hands on my thighs. My skin is still a little cool and his is so warm, so delightfully warm against my body.

"Have to? Samantha." He kisses my thighs, his hands stroking and gently nudging my legs apart. "This is my pleasure." He lifts my hips and tugs my underwear down my legs. I gasp as he yanks them all the way off and tosses them over a shoulder as he situates himself between my legs. His hands and lips are everywhere—except where I'm growing increasingly desperate for them to be. My mind races, thinking of all the things I should be doing, of how he probably doesn't actually want to be doing this.

"Samantha." He takes my hand and presses a kiss to my palm, setting it on his shoulder. "I want to do this. I want to make you feel good. I want this very much, beautiful."

"Oooh." I think my spinal column explodes when he calls me beautiful. My body collapses into the couch as he finally dips a tongue between my legs, his mouth hot and so wet, his touch delicious on my needy skin. I keep my hand where he placed it and drop the other hand into his hair, burying my fingers in his messy, dark mop as AJ licks and strokes my body.

My hips rock up to meet his mouth and he groans in approval, goading me on as I thrust against his knuckle. "You taste amazing," he moans, "Exactly perfect." I don't have time to doubt him because I start coming on his tongue. I gasp and jolt, digging my hands into his body as waves of pleasure break through me. The room fills with light and my head snaps back as my orgasm rolls on and on. Somewhere I hear his voice encouraging me. "Yes, Sam. Just like that. God, you're so sexy when you come for me." He presses the heel of one hand against my clit as I spasm around one of his fingers.

I don't know how much time passes, or if I passed out or what, but when I gain awareness of my surroundings, AJ is kneeling in front of me, tucking my robe back into place and groaning a bit as he stands. Somewhere in the house, I hear the buzzer of the dryer finishing its cycle. He grins. "I should let you get back to work."

Before I can protest he jogs up the stairs and when I see him next, he's tucking in his shirt with his picnic blanket draped over one shoulder. He comes back in the living room and sits on the arm of the couch, leaning forward and kissing the top of my head. "Are you going to be okay or did I break you?"

That makes me laugh and snaps me a little bit out of my orgasm-coma. "It will take more than one of those to break me, Trachtenberg."

He grins again, a crooked half-smile. "I'm up for the challenge of seeing what pushes you over the edge."

I groan and let my head flop back. "This public offering. That's what's going to push me over the edge. If I even get that far."

AJ starts tying his shoes. "What do you mean?"

I shrug. "There's been a lot of bad press about me lately. Did you see the article in *Forbes*?"

He laughs. "I'm not sure what made you think I'm the kind of guy who reads *Forbes*."

"Fair. Well, they basically implied I'm a huge ditz."

AJ frowns. "That couldn't be further from the truth."

"Well, thank you, and I know that. But…" I flip my hair back out of my eyes and gesture at my piles of work. "Let's just say I need all the good news puff pieces I can get right now. I wouldn't hate it if your school bragged about me on social media, for instance…"

As soon as I say it, I know it's the wrong thing to say. AJ purses his lips and his demeanor shifts. "I should go," he repeats, standing.

I bite my lip. "I didn't mean I expect that. That's not why I made the bird page for you."

He nods. "I know. But thank you for saying so. And I really should get going."

"I really should let you."

He looks at me for a few beats, nods, and turns. When I hear the door click shut I can't help but worry that my big mouth just messed up the best thing I've had going for me in a   long,   long   while.

CHAPTER TWENTY-SEVEN

AJ

My sister calls as I'm driving to work. I groan when I see her name come up, knowing I was the topic of family dinner conversation last night. "Good morning, Avi."

"So Bubbie says you're getting married." She cuts right to the point. I appreciate that as I need to go inside and certainly don't want this conversation overheard.

"Yep, Av, and she's expecting twins, too. Did she mention that part?"

My sister laughs. "So is there anything to this or has Bubs been huffing glue at yenta craft hour?"

I sigh. "There's a woman. It's…new." She squeals. "Please do not squeal."

"AJ, do you realize what this means?"

"This means nothing. This means I'm seeing someone."

"You took her to temple and she met Bubbie." My sister blows a raspberry. "That ain't nothing."

"Look, Avi, I just pulled up at work. I can't have middle schoolers overhearing this conversation."

"I'm surprised they don't know already, what with Bubbie taking out an ad in the newspaper."

"She did not."

"Adriel Trachtenberg is officially moving on after the ice bitch stabbed him in the heart."

"Come on, Avi, please."

"All right, all right." My sister sighs. "Can I meet her?"

"Goodbye, Avi." I hang up before she can come back at me. I don't get long to recover, though, because Leo and Doug are waiting for me outside the door.

"You're really putting me through the gauntlet," I groan, but then I perk up when Doug offers me a wax paper bundle.

"My sister in law made scones," he says. "I'll trade you for details about date night."

I gesture for the pastries as Leo groans that it's not fair since he didn't get any carbs. "How did you two even know about date night?" Leo swipes his badge to get us in the door and we make our way up to the teachers' lounge to drop off our lunches.

Leo looks at me strangely. "You were going on and on about the bird watching," he says. "You absolutely never take that sort of stance on being the one to do recon on a potential student project."

"And how exactly does that translate to date night?"

Doug pushes open the door to the lounge and clicks on the lights. "You telling us you didn't take a certain data analyst along with you to count birds?"

I sigh. "Fine." I unfold the wax paper and the buttery scent of the scones fills the room. Leo's stomach growls. I snap it in half and hand it to my friend as I tell them most of the details of my night with Samantha.

Doug is grinning like he just won a contest or something. "I'm really happy for you, man. This is giving me life this week. Did I tell you my oldest needs to start wearing deodorant? Things are not okay for me at home."

Leo wipes his hands on a paper towel as he finishes chewing the end of his portion of scone. "But something's off," he says. "Your shoulders are practically up at your ears."

"I'm not tense," I say, as I consciously lower my shoulders and roll my neck, trying to relax.

"What happened," Leo asks, leaning against the copy machine and then jumping when his hip causes it to whir awake.

I take a bite of the scone, trying to decide how to tell them about the niggling fear eating at me, that Samantha is using my students to bolster her reputation. Using me, too. I dab a napkin at my stubble, which has almost progressed into beard territory. "She's having some issues with work. Something about bad press."

Doug's eyebrows fly up. "I read that article, actually. That reporter seems like a jackass. The whole thing felt uncalled for."

I nod. "Sam says the IPO is at risk now, that the board is questioning her leadership in response to all the articles."

A clattering sound comes from outside the room and the three of us turn our heads to the hall. Margot pokes her head into the room, trailing a backpack so heavy she pulls it on wheels like luggage. "Sorry. I got here early to meet with Mr. Rogers about proofreading my profile for the coding camp…"

Doug nods and grins. "I remember, Margot. Let's go take a look."

She hesitates. "Mr. T, did you say Samantha is having trouble with Vinea?"

I scowl. But if Doug is reading the media, it's not like Margot won't just go do an internet search. "There was a negative article about her company, yes. But I'm sure she and her staff will overcome this."

"Can we do anything to help? She did so much for us." Margot squeezes her backpack handle so tightly her fingers turn white.

"Nothing for you to worry about, Margot. I'm sure Ms. Vine wants you to focus on school."

She nods and follows Doug out of the room. I listen as their voices trail off when they arrive at his classroom. Leo slides in next to where I'm leaning against the counter. "What's really eating you about what Sam said?"

My heart races and I close my eyes. I feel like I want to just tamp down this hunch, as if saying it out loud will call it to life. "Just…echoes of Lara, I guess."

Leo snorts. "Sam isn't Lara, dude."

I purse my lips. "She'd do anything for this company, though, and if the board is having concerns…"

"Okay, ask yourself this. Would a woman sit with you in the rain to count birds if she was using you to finagle good press?"

I shrug. "I don't fucking know, man. Clearly I don't have a good track record understanding women's motives. I shouldn't even be allowed to try."

Leo pats me on the back. "Don't say that, AJ. You're a catch. Remember that." I roll my eyes. "I'm serious. And she's a catch, too. I'm glad you caught each other."

"Thanks, Leo."

"Don't mention it. Now." He rubs his palms together. "Let's say we play rock, paper, scissors for who has to proctor recess this week."

I laugh. "No way. I'm department head. I have responsibilities. Recess detail is for *regular* teachers."

"There it is," he says, pointing at me. "There's the grouchy bastard we know and love."

CHAPTER TWENTY-EIGHT

Samantha

More Trouble at the Helm of Vinea: Board Questions Vine's Leadership
  Pittsburgh Business Herald

Can Vine Swing a Public Company?
  Tech Daily

I ask Audrey to stop sending me headlines. They're starting to impact my focus, and I need to stay sharp as we onboard our new team members this week. Audrey and Shane seem to have that part under control, though. I feel like an audience member as I sit in the overview meetings with our new marketing and business strategy execs. What I really want to do is dig back into the software. AJ's bird project got me thinking of all the potential partnerships out there with citizen science organizations. We could offer free access to Vinea for these folks to track data, tease out correlations.

My phone buzzes in my lap. A text from AJ. I notice my stomach flutter at the thought of him. Or is that an impending heart attack? ***Are you free for dinner tonight?***

I bite my lip. I'm not free. Not at all. But I want to be. *I could make time for a quick bite,* I text back. *Maybe someplace near Vinea?*

Want me to bring tacos to you at your office?
Oh my god I love that idea!
Good. See you at 6.

I can't stop smiling as we wrap up the meetings. I even smile as I sift through contracts with new clients, and that part generally tends to make me nervous. Despite the headlines recently, we've landed a few new partnerships with companies researching new vaccines. It thrills me to no end to think my company might play some small role in helping to eradicate a disease like Lyme.

I'm still riding that high hours later when I hear a tap on my door and look up to see AJ leaning against my door frame, wearing his typical sweater with collared shirt and tie, looking dark and hairy and delicious. "Hey," I say. And then I smell the tacos. "Oh my god, get in here with those." My stomach starts gurgling. "I think I skipped lunch."

"That's not good," he says, sitting in a chair at the round table in the center of the room. Which means I have to get up and walk away from my computer to get to the tacos. My joints creak as I stand. He frowns. "How much are you working, Sam?"

I shrug and reach for a brown paper bag. "A lot." I pull out the tray from Baby Loves Tacos, gleefully assembling the soft tortilla with spiced meat and corn salsa and pickled cabbage. "It's just until the IPO," I say around my mouthful of food. I'm so hungry I don't even care that he's looking at me drip food all over the place. I note that he somehow manages to eat his taco in tidy bites. "You shaved," I say, reaching my hand across the table to feel his cheek.

He nods. "It was time." I mock a frown at that and he laughs. "It can be a beard again in a few hours. Any time you want."

I wink at him. "I always want." The phone on my desk rings and I groan. All the admin staff have left for the day. "I have to get that," I whine and he nods. When I pick up the receiver, Logan's voice comes frantically through the line.

"Samantha, you need to call General Watson right now. They're threatening to end their contract."

"Wait." I set down my taco and wipe my hand on my skirt. "What?" Logan repeats herself and explains that the military contract is apparently at risk in response to the recent bad press.

"Their lawyer said something about a good faith clause? I don't even know. You need to call him."

"Text me the—"

"Already sent you the number. Call from the office phone."

I glance over at AJ. "This is going to take just a few minutes," I tell him. He nods and continues eating his taco. I dial the line and wait until I hear the deep, stern voice of one of our biggest new clients. "General Watson, this is Samantha Vine from Vinea. How are you this evening?"

"Well, Ms. Vine, not great, if we're being honest."

"Logan tells me you're having some concerns about our contract?"

He spits out the expected response to the relentless headlines that have been questioning my leadership lately. "And further, you failed to reveal your personal connection to Colonel Vine here at my own god damned military base. When I spoke to him he didn't even seem too aware of our partnership."

I sigh and sink into my desk chair. "General, may I be frank?" AJ arches a brow and watches me, continuing to eat his taco and making me very hungry.

"Please." The general clears his throat.

"My father wasn't aware of our business particulars because I keep my personal life separate from my work. I would hope you would appreciate that discretion, as someone with security clearance."

He grunts. "It makes me wonder what else you haven't

revealed."

I frown. "General, I'm the architect of this software. I sought you out personally because of the unprecedented data set available via your service members. Your top researchers agree with me that our partnership can be essential to keeping your forces battle-ready. How many enlisted folks did you have out with Lyme disease last summer after training exercises? With sexually transmitted infections? Vinea is partnering with the institutions looking to solve these health crises."

"Hmm." I hear him moving around in his desk chair.

"My father hasn't let my mother's death or even his recent cataract surgery impact his work. Don't let clickbait headlines persuade you. I'm ready to grow this company. Sir."

There's a long silence in which AJ chews and stares at me and the general says nothing. Until he says, "Well I was not aware that Colonel Vine was a widower."

"It's been a long time, sir. Like I said, we Vines keep our personal lives separate from our work."

He coughs. "I appreciate you taking the time to call me about this issue."

I sag in relief. "I appreciate the opportunity to reassure you we are the real deal."

"Have a good night, Ms. Vine." He hangs up.

I set the phone in the receiver and begin to massage my temples. And then I feel hands on my shoulders. I look up to find AJ standing behind me, his big palms kneading my muscles. I melt. "Do you want to talk about it?" His voice is gentle, no hint of sarcasm or pointed digs. I shake my head. He starts to rub my scalp and I moan. "I'm sorry you lost your mother. Will you tell me about her?"

I smile and being to purr as his fingers press into the tense skin all over my head and neck and shoulders. He's good at this. "Her name was Liza. She did everything for us."

"Liza Vine," he murmurs.

"And when she died, someone had to do all the things."

"Let me guess," he presses a kiss to the top of my head. "That someone has been you." I nod. "So you do all the things for your family, and you do all the things here."

"I'm very good at doing things."

"Mm hmm." His voice is so low, so soothing. I'm about to fall asleep right here. "Except remembering to feed yourself and stand up often enough that your knees don't creak."

"Paging Dr. Trachtenberg," I joke. "Your patient is ignoring her health."

He chuckles and keeps kneading. "Dr. Trachtenberg is my father. And my grandfather. And my aunt."

I turn my head slightly to see him better. "But not you?" He shakes his head. I close my eyes. "You're great with your students. They're lucky to have you."

"Thank you," he whispers, giving me a final squeeze. "You look like you could fall asleep right here."

I rest my head back against the chair. "I'll sleep when I'm retired."

"What if I drive you home and you sleep right now?" He walks around the chair and squats on the floor in front of me, his face etched with concern.

I shake my head. "There are only a few weeks left. I've got to find a way to reassure the board that I'm on this. I can't have contracts like the U.S. fucking Military threatening to pull funds." All the relaxation from AJ's touch is slipping away rapidly. "I have to call Logan back and then I have to go over all these notes for the vaccine researchers." I gesture around the room.

AJ scowls. "How will you get home? You don't seem like you're in a great headspace to drive."

I shrug. "I've slept on my office couch before."

"Samantha."

I hold up a hand, stand, and stride back over to my taco. Even with the long delay, it's still an explosion of amazing flavor in my mouth. I almost cry, it tastes so good. I swallow my bite. "You brought me dinner and massaged my neck and that was fucking amazing. And now I have to get back to work."

He puts his hands in his pockets and looks around the room, hesitating. Finally, he nods. "I'd like to see you again. Soon."

I close my eyes. I have no idea how I can make that happen and still salvage my business reputation. I really need to talk with Shane and the marketing team about some sort of PR defense. Shit. AJ is still waiting for me to answer him. "I'll try," I tell him. "This weekend?"

He nods, kisses my cheek, and walks out of the office.

CHAPTER TWENTY-NINE

AJ

My family is going to murder me. They've said so, repeatedly. They thought I was bringing Samantha to dinner after services and…I didn't want to overwhelm her with everything going on at work, so I didn't bring it up.

Avi glares at me as she scoops potatoes onto her plate. Angry potato scooping, if that's a thing. Bubbie squeezes my father's hand as she laments, "You should see this girl! The most beautiful woman I've ever seen in my life—apart from you and Avi, of course." My mother and sister wave away her remark, hanging on her words. Bubbie arches a brow. "Of course, if the three of you made more of an effort to get to the synagogue, you'd know what she looks like, wouldn't you?" I chuckle at her ability to weave guilt into every conversation, for everyone in the room. Bubbie points a fork at me. "I shouldn't let you have brisket, Adriel. Imagine that poor woman sitting all alone, starving."

I roll my eyes at that. "She's an adult with a career, Bubbie. She ate dinner on her own long before she met me."

To my surprise, my mother joins Bubbie with a stern expression. "That's exactly the point, Adriel John. She was on her own, and now she's with you."

Avi nods. "Yeah, bro. She's missing out on the opportunity for Mom to show her pictures from your bris."

Mom tries not to laugh but ends up snorting her wine. Dad's shoulders shake as he tries not to laugh. My parents absolutely did pull out that specific photo album to show my prom date. I sigh. The truth is I'm feeling really confused about Samantha. I no longer think she'd consciously use my students as a PR opportunity for her company, but I'm not convinced she wouldn't do so unintentionally.

Then I have other moments of confusion. When she was on the phone with that military guy, expertly handling him, oozing competence and confidence, I found myself once again drowning in my own feelings of inadequacy. Until Samantha turned those big, brown eyes at me and told me she thinks I'm an amazing teacher, like she might actually mean it. She didn't seem to care that I didn't follow the family career path. I curse Lara under my breath, wondering if it counts as progress that I can at least recognize that my response is due to her words and actions.

With these thoughts swirling, I eat my meal silently while my family argues about my shortcomings in not bringing a date to family dinner. I don't usually bring my phone with me to meals—or anywhere, really. But I have it in my pocket today, and I feel a surge of emotion when it vibrates with a message. Glancing down, I see that it's from Samantha.

You made me feel really good the other night. I grin, trying to return my phone to my pocket before my family notices me acting like a middle schooler. I've taught enough of them to know it's obvious when someone is lap texting. But then another message comes in and I feel my heart squeeze. ***This is me being vulnerable, telling you I had a hard fucking day and you made me feel better.***

The truth is I had no idea what to do when I saw her so visibly upset. Bringing dinner was easy—everyone likes tacos. But then I had to sit there listening to a booming male voice question her authority and her business leadership. I felt powerless, and then I felt an overwhelming urge to touch her.

153

Not in a sexual way, but just to somehow let her know I…care about her. Fuck. I care about Samantha Vine. More than care.

I close my eyes tightly, trying to ward off the stream of thoughts that were about to envision a future with her, glimpses of her actually seated around this table trading witticisms with my mother and then curled in bed with me, her clacking away on her laptop as I read or graded papers. "No," I say out loud, before I can catch myself, and my sister narrows her eyes at me.

"No? Like, no you're never bringing her to dinner or just no, not next week?" I hadn't realized they'd continued discussing Samantha's Trachtenberg family debut. I shake my head. "I don't know. It's all very new." I look at my plate of half-eaten food, my appetite slipping away. I look up at my mother and say, "She's not even Jewish."

Mom smiles and squeezes my father's hand. He shrugs. Bubbie leans back in her chair like I just revealed something shocking. Which, I guess I did. Mom takes a swig of her wine and says, "The heart wants what it wants, AJ." I feel a weight lift and I realize I've been dreading telling my family about this aspect of Samantha.

My relief is short-lived when Bubbie snorts and says, "Well, she can always convert," which sets off a series of explosive shouts from my father and sister. I grin when Avi calls Bubbie a "nebby old yenta." I never really thought my family would be unsupportive of anyone I dated, but it's nice to hear my parents and sister sticking up for Samantha, even if I still don't know where things are heading with her.

Suddenly the enormity of this conversation exhausts me and I feel a strong impulse to leave. "I'm sorry, but I have to go grade papers. I wish I could stay longer."

That last part's a lie. Sort of. I stand up to find my mother behind me with her arms out, wrapping me in a jiggling, squeezing hug. "Are you going to invite me in for career day this year?" She taps my chin and looks into my eyes, reaching up to brush my hair back from my face. "You work too much."

I laugh. "This from the woman who hasn't taken a day off in years."

She swats my shoulder and I kiss her on the forehead, clap my father on the cheek, and deposit my plate in the kitchen. When I turn around, Bubbie is standing near me with a frown and her arms laden with repurposed margarine containers. "Adriel John," she scolds. "You go take that woman some food."

"Bubs, I told you, I have to grade—"

My grandmother presses a gnarled finger to my lips. "There's matzo ball soup here, Adriel. Everyone needs matzo ball soup." I sigh and accept Bubbie's peace offering. I really should go home and grade papers. But once again I find myself unable to resist the urge to understand more about the swirl of emotions and confusion that light up my brain whenever I think of Samantha Vine.

I drive to her house, knowing I have to deliver the soup, and smile when I see that she's got her heavy front door open to allow the breeze through her screen door. It doesn't occur to me that she might not be alone in there until I strut up the walk, raise my fist to rap on the door, and hear a chorus of cackles   from   inside.

CHAPTER THIRTY
Samantha

Of course Esther would have Bridges and Bitters closed for deep cleaning this afternoon when I need her most. Thankfully I was able to convince some members of Foof to come to my house for an emergency meeting. To listen to me implode.

I beg Esther to bring drinks, order way too much food for delivery, and drape myself across my couch like a regency-era duchess in need of smelling salts. Nicole, Orla, and Logan arrive first, telling me they're skipping some sort of torturous family running event.

Chloe comes bearing heaps of glossy photographs of potential cover models for us to help her "research" and Piper arrives with Esther, each of them carrying giant glass jugs of alcohol.

Piper slams hers onto my hardwood floor and points a sweaty finger at me. "Only for your crisis would I skip a workout today. It's gorgeous outside!"

Esther nods. "Are you sure you don't want to walk by a river or something?"

I shake my head and point at the pile of newspaper clippings on my coffee table. "I can't risk someone taking my picture and trying to spin me as someone shirking responsibilities to go galavanting."

Logan groans. "You told Audrey to stop sending you clippings and here you are obsessing over them alone? Sam!" She squeezes my leg. "You need to ignore these assholes."

Nicole wedges herself onto the couch beside me, resting a hand over her stomach. "Someone catch me up. I've had my head in a toilet for three months while this lichen takes root."

Orla snickers at her but says, "The media has it out for Sam, and it's giving her board the heebie jeebies going into their initial public offering." She looks at Logan. "Did I call it the right thing?" Logan nods.

Nicole frowns. She works as a business strategist and has experience taking a company public in the past. I tried to hire her a year ago but she's committed to her current job. "Your marketing team should really have a plan for this, Sam. What are they submitting to various media outlets?"

My head flops back against the couch as I mutter about only recently acquiring a real marketing staff. Chloe hands me a glass and I take a swig of the sweet, boozy contents. "I don't even like this aspect of...everything." I gesture toward my front door. "Honest to god, all I want to do is lock myself in a cave with 3 monitors and code something fantastic.".

Logan pats my leg. "You already did that, babe. And people love it! And it's about to get easier for people to access it. You'll see."

"Hm." I take another swig. "Esther, you delightful witch. This is amazing."

She smiles. "I'm trying this out for pumpkin spice season."

I take another swig and frown. "I don't taste anything pumpkiny, though..."

Esther cackles. "Because I fucking hate pumpkin spice. Everyone knows the apple is the star of the show in autumn." Everyone laughs. "That's an Autumn Pimm's Cup with brandy, local apple cider, sliced apples from the same orchard, oranges, and a cinnamon stick."

I'm about to comment when I hear a tap on my screen

door. I turn my head to see none other than Adriel Trachtenberg biting his lip on my stoop. I wonder how much he heard, feeling sheepish about him knowing I haven't been loving my role as CEO. That was information for Foof ears only.

I'm about to get up and let him in when Chloe beats me to the punch, springing up from the couch and squealing. "You were at my release party," she says to him. She clutches his hand. "Thank you so much for your support. Truly."

He arches a brow at her. "My pleasure," he grunts, with no joy whatsoever. It makes me laugh. He clears his throat. "I'm sorry for barging in. I didn't mean to crash your party."

Nicole and Orla stand up and start clearing away glasses. Nicole looks AJ up and down and says, "We were just leaving anyway."

"What? You absolutely were not leaving." I grab the neck of the bottle before Piper hauls it away. Chloe and Esther grab one of the paper bags of food. "We're going for that walk," Piper says. "As the resident fitness expert, I need to look out for my friends' cardiovascular health."

"But I don't want to walk." I pout and take another swig of my Pimm's Cup.

Esther grins. "We know you don't, babe." She pats AJ on the shoulder. "We'll leave you here with this guy."

Before he can protest and before I can convince them otherwise, Foof has faded out of the house without a trace. Except for the glass bottle of hooch I'm cradling in my lap like a baby. Eventually, AJ deposits a plastic grocery bag on my coffee table, sinks into the couch beside me and grips my thigh, sending heat soaring to my crotch.

"I was worried you'd still be in your office," he says, giving me a small smile.

I shake my head. "I came home eventually." He gestures for the alcohol and I hand him the jug.

He takes a sip and his eyebrows shoot up. "This is

delicious."

"Isn't it? Esther is so good at what she does."

We pass the jug back and forth a few times before he says, "My family is angry with me because I didn't bring you to dinner today."

I sigh. "I probably would have been a distraction today anyway. So much going on." I gesture around vaguely and he nods. "Isn't it early for dinner, though? What time is it?"

He stretches out on the couch and drapes an arm around my shoulders. I surprise myself by instinctively curling in closer to him, like a magnet snapping into place on the fridge. "Is there a better vocabulary word for late lunch? We ate at my parents' house after services."

"Lupper? Dunch?"

"Definitely not dunch." He starts stroking my hair and it's almost enough to make me forget all the stress of this week. All the stress of last night. "How long until this all wraps up for you?" He tilts his head so I can feel his breath on my skin as he talks.

"Supposed to be this week."

"Want to know what I think?"

I press a hand against his chest and push back a little so I can see his whole face. "Actually, no. I don't want to talk about work at all, if that's okay."

He gives a small smile. "That's definitely okay." And then he leans in to kiss me. I realize this is what I've been hoping for, or needing at any rate. I moan in relief as he deepens the kiss, one of his hands cradling my cheek.

"I want to have dirty, rough, hairy sex," I tell him, nipping at his finger, which he withdraws as his eyes widen. Those eyes darken as he nods his head. I yelp when he wraps my ponytail around his fist and tugs, tilting my head back. "Yes," I groan as he licks my throat.

"Get upstairs," he growls and I feel a rush of excitement. I don't have to decide anything, because he's telling me what to do right now, and he's taking off his shirt.

"Fuck, yes," I whoop, scampering up the stairs as he chases after me, shedding his clothes along the way. When we get to my room he shoves me against the wall, kissing me as his hands are rough along my boobs. "I wish you had a ruler," I pant. "I want you to rap my knuckles with it."

He pauses. "You understand corporal punishment is illegal now, right?"

I roll my eyes. "You're fucking up my fantasy, Adriel."

He arches a brow and says, "Hmmm." He slides his belt out from the loops on his pants and smacks his left palm with the leather. My eyes fly wide. He grins. "Too much. Got it." He tosses the belt over his shoulder and spins me around so I'm facing the wall. In a few yanks and tugs, he's got my ass exposed as my palms press into the pale blue paint.

I gasp when he slaps my ass, the crack echoing through my townhouse. His fingertips massage my skin as he cups my cheek where his palm stung a moment before. "How's this for a fantasy?" AJ's voice is low in my ear and I swallow in anticipation, waiting to see what he'll do next. Loving that I don't know.

He draws his hand back and slaps the other cheek and I whimper in pleasure, especially when his fingers cup between my legs, drawing my moisture along my body as he massages. His teeth sink into the skin beneath my ear and I feel his fingers everywhere at once—he rubs them along my nipples, my stomach, my ass, but never my clit. "Please, AJ," I beg. I feel a desperate throb between my legs as my clit longs for his attention.

From over my shoulder, I hear AJ crinkling a condom wrapper and then I feel a steadying hand on my hip before a swell of pressure between my legs as he sinks inside me. I release a guttural moan, melting into the wall, my nipples loving the friction against the matte finish as AJ settles his cock inside me.

"Holy fuck, you feel perfect," he grunts, and then he starts to thrust. Slowly at first, he slides in and out while he traces all his little teeth marks with his fingertips. At least I imagine he can see them, illuminated like stars along my skin. Or burn marks where he has seared into my central nervous system.

My palms slide against the wall, slick with sweat as my body wriggles, seeking friction. "You need to come, don't you?" He tugs my hair again and turns my head so I can see his eyes. I nod as much as I can with my hair around his wrist and he grins, a wicked flash among his dark hair. AJ slides his hand to my crotch and barely touches me before I come, pulsing and squeezing around the massive invasion of his thick cock.

"Fuck," we say together. "Yes." I moan and come and start to slide down the wall. Once I'm on my knees he backs up and hauls me up against his chest, pounding into me a few more times before he howls and I feel him come. Heaving, panting, exhausted, we both crumple to the floor in my room. When I look up at the wall, I see sweat marks from my boobs, and we laugh, both of us thrilled by this memento.

It's nearly dark when I hear my phone ringing from somewhere downstairs. I lift my head from the fuzzy pillow of AJ's chest and frown. I really don't want to get out of bed, but I'm probably too close to the IPO to ignore calls, even on a weekend.

AJ groans as I try to slither out of bed. He reaches for me feebly, but I grab his t-shirt and slide it on as I head down my steps. I find my phone on the coffee table. I've missed several calls already from Shane and Audrey, and now it's Logan trying to get through. "What," I say. "I'm here. Sorry!"

"Eep! Sam!" Logan is in full excite mode. I take a seat to prepare myself for her news. "You've gone viral."

"I was already viral. Remember? Blonde bimbo tries to do business blah blah…"

"No," she sounds assertive. "Good viral. I'm sending you a link. Keep me on speaker when you pull it up."

I squint and navigate to my messages as the phone bings in my hand. Logan sends a link to the video of the Franklin Middle School students thanking Vinea for the field trip. It looks like an extended version of the video—more than what I had seen. I smile as the kids ham for the camera and joke about their data analysis.

Logan says, "They included a hashtag. Learn with Vinea! And it's trending."

"Really?" I smile. On speaker, Logan talks about some of the commentary she's finding online about the impact companies like Vinea can have on public education. I almost cry, I'm so touched.

But then I hear something behind me and I look over my shoulder to see AJ. And he's not happy.

"Hey, Logan, I have to go. But thank you for sending this to me, okay?"

"Absolutely, Sam. Audrey and Shane wanted me to assure you that the marketing team and the community engagement staff is on it."

She clicks off and I sigh, until I realize that AJ is really, steaming mad. He grips the couch as he stands behind me barefoot in his slacks. "Where did you get that video?"

"Logan just texted it to me."

He points to my phone. "You assured me that you would not share that content. And now it's gone viral?"

I swallow and start to shake my head. "AJ, it's not the same video. Look, let me show you—"

"This is so unacceptable, Samantha. These are children. Not pawns in your PR adventure."

I furrow my brow at him. "PR adventure? You know I've been under intense scrutiny that is often unfair and untrue."

"Oh I know all about it. And you had an ace in your sleeve, didn't you? A way to save face when everyone was picking apart your leadership abilities. Nevermind that you had to lie and steal footage of minors without parental permission!" AJ shoves his bare feet into his shoes and bends over to pick up his button-down. He fumbles with the buttons and looks around for his keys, snatching them and his phone off my coffee table.

"Where are you going?"

"Back to my apartment to call my boss and figure out the legal ramifications of your little stunt."

I stand up and glare at him. "You have no right to speak to me this way and you cannot just storm out of here every time you get mad!"

He rolls his eyes at me like I'm one of his middle schoolers. "I should have never been over here to get mad to begin with. Women like you are only looking to get ahead, and I don't know what it will take for me to learn that once and for all."

He strides toward the door and I hurry to insert myself in his way. "Women like me? What the fuck is that supposed to mean?" I think back to how stiff he got when his grandmother brought up his ex at the synagogue. "I don't like being compared to your past asshole girlfriends when I have done nothing wrong here. All I've been is honest with you."

He throws his hands in the air. "You're right. You've been very honest that your top priority is your company and guiding it to this next phase. Congratulations, Samantha. You did it. And you got some good dick along the way. Good night."

When I don't move out of the way, he growls and marches through the kitchen, out my back door, and through the side gate before I crumple to the floor in shocked silence.

CHAPTER THIRTY-ONE
AJ

From: Vinelli, Kellie
Sent: Monday, October 9
To: [All Staff]
Subj: Morning Middle School Memo!

Good Morning Faculty! Just a quick reminder that many of our students' guardians have NOT signed photo release forms! Please do not share images (including video) of your students online in any capacity! This includes field trips!
Have a great day On Purpose!
Kellie Vinelli, Principal

I'm right back where I was last year. No. I'm worse off than that. Not only have I let myself believe a woman could have feelings for me, again, but now I also have to meet with my perky boss and problem-solve a social media disaster. I wonder if I need to call my union rep…

Unable to stand being alone with my thoughts a second longer, I drive in to work obscenely early on Monday. Where I am, of course, also alone with my thoughts. And the smell of adolescent feet. I try grading papers at my desk, but the sound of my pen scraping along exams irritates me. Everything irritates me, from terrible teachers' lounge coffee to the feel of ball-point pen on copy paper, to Samantha fucking Vine using me as a prop to bolster her image in the press.

I stand up and hurl my pen and hear someone laugh when it clatters to the ground. I turn my head to see Doug leaning against my door frame, munching a donut. He points at me. "Any idea what prompted Vinelli's latest memo?"

I frown at him and walk over to pick up my pen. Doug walks into the room and sits on top of one of the student desks. He offers me a donut. I frown at it, but accept it when he continues to shake the donut at me. I don't even like donuts, but I eat most of it before I even realize I'm doing so. He pulls a travel coffee mug from the crook of his arm and slurps it for a bit while I brood.

"Samantha's been using me," I finally mutter, and then close my eyes because I hate how it feels to say that out loud.

Doug sighs. "Tell me why you think so."

I press my palms to my desk and I feel my nostrils flare. "So you haven't seen the viral video of our students, shilling for her company? She's been crafting this for months." My mind spirals as I blurt all my dark assumptions to Doug. "Her snap instinct was to have nothing to do with our students, and then she relentlessly demands we go there for a field trip? Her team must have seen us coming a mile away."

Doug taps his fingers on the desk. "But didn't our kids reveal that they were the ones who made that video? Not her or anyone from Vinea?"

I roll my eyes. "Yeah, they made the video on devices conveniently donated by Vinea. She's probably got trackers on all of them, mining all the kids' data for her cloud or whatever it's fucking called."

Doug stares at me and I slump back in my seat. He says, "AJ, you're really assuming the worst here. I saw the two of you together at the book party…she didn't look like a woman using people for her own gain."

I roll my eyes. "Back then she was just trying to get into my pants."

This gets a laugh out of both of us. Doug leans forward and the desk tips a little. He rights himself and shakes his head. "Sometimes people like doing things for other people. There's that whole theory about love languages...acts of service..."

I snort. "Service makes her feel shitty. She's been doing service for her entire family for years. All kinds of shit for her siblings that they should do for their own damn adult selves."

"Like drive her grandmother to church every week?"

"What's that supposed to mean? And you know it's not called church."

He holds his hands up. "Sorry. Synagogue. But AJ, do you drive your grandmother out of obligation? Do you resent it? Do you have ulterior motives in researching citizen science projects for your kids to pursue?" He raises a brow and I growl at him.

Just then, Leo saunters into the room shaking his cell phone. "Saw Vinelli's email, dude. Then I saw the video. Hashtag Learn with Vinca!"

"Shut the fuck up, Leo." As soon as I say it I wince. "I'm sorry." I dig my fingers into my hair and tug, groaning.

Leo looks at me, then looks to Doug, who says, "He's back to thinking Sam had ulterior motives in humping him."

Leo cackles. "Humping! I think the kids are calling it vibing right now, right?" Doug shrugs. Leo turns to me and sits on the edge of my desk. "Look, this is about Lara and you know it, AJ." Turning to Doug, Leo says, "His ex left him because she's a gold digger and it fucked with his head."

"That sucks, man. But I don't think you have to worry about that with Samantha..."

My eyes flash when I look up. "Oh no? You don't think she's also using me to get ahead? Remember the viral student video where the kids' parents didn't sign release forms?

Causing me to have to sit in a room with exclamation-point-Vinelli?"

Leo starts shaking his head and running a hand across his throat and I look past his shoulder to see Margot standing in the door to my room. She looks like she's been crying. "Mr. T?" Margot wrings her hands.

"Margot. I'm sorry you had to hear some of that. What can I do for you?"

Doug and Leo act like they're getting ready to leave but they take their sweet time about it, so I know I'm not going to get out of talking through this with them. I take a deep breath as Margot approaches my desk. "I think I did a bad thing."

Leo arches a brow and Doug leans forward. She looks between them and back to me. "Me and some of the kids were talking…about how I heard you say Ms. Vine is getting a bad shake in the media." She bites her lip and rocks up on her tiptoes. "We wanted to help and show people how awesome she is."

Doug whistles. Leo moon walks out of my classroom. I stare at Margot for a few beats. "Margot, nobody is angry. But what did you do? Specifically?"

She bites her lip again and fidgets with her hair. She shrugs. "We added some stuff to that thank you video we made and then…" She swallows and shrugs again. "We all posted it online."

CHAPTER THIRTY-TWO
Samantha

Vinea jumps to $38 billion market cap as public investors get their first crack at the popular data analysis solution
Investor Daily News
Vinea Stock Continues To Climb on Day 1 of Trading
Stock Sense

Audrey beams as she calls the executive leadership meeting to order. I'm so proud of her and grateful for all she's done for this company. And me. I feel my eyes well up a bit as she says, "I'm so excited to gather here with a full roster on such an important day. I cannot wait to see what we all achieve together."

In the past month, Audrey, Logan and Shane have set up entire teams in marketing, Human Resources, finance, and business development. That last one makes me feel the most grateful, even as it makes me clench my jaw. I'm working really hard on admitting to myself that delegating these tasks is a sign of success. This is still my company, even if I'd rather hole up with my tech team and continue developing our products.

"We've had some amazing feedback from our board of directors," Audrey continues. "Major kudos to our marketing team for propping up the recent social media excitement about Vinea! Sam, do you want to be the one to share the good news with the group?"

I press my lips together. I'm still sort of waiting for someone to say they're just kidding and the SEC said no thanks to Vinea joining the stock market. "Shouldn't this be Logan's time to shine? She did most of the work on this."

Logan shakes her head and pats my hand. "Go on, Sam. Say it out loud. Say the words."

I look around the table at my friends, and colleagues I hope will soon be my friends. All I've wanted for so long was to create a place where everyone felt like their work is valued and seen. I take a deep breath and glance at the sticky note I've been clutching since Logan met me at my office door this morning. "Well," I swallow. "About 16 million shares of Vinea stock will begin trading on Wednesday morning."

The room erupts in cheers and everyone stands, walking around to pat me on the back and hug one another.

When all the shouting dies down, I notice Logan and Shane calling their spouses. Audrey video chats her mom. I feel a wave of grief wash over me. My family doesn't even know this is happening and my mother…I honestly can't remember enough about her to guess how she'd respond to this news. My thoughts drift briefly to AJ's hands on my shoulders, the feel of his furry chest against my cheek. He'd probably take me out to dinner if he didn't think I was—I'm not actually sure what it is AJ thinks of me. I step out of the conference room and tackle some emails ahead of the wave I know is coming. At least I can save my new assistant and marketing team a little busywork that way.

The work day is a blur of questions and joyful conversations. Logan leads an information session with the entire staff explaining how many shares of the company they'll each get and what they are and are not allowed to do with them the first day. I feel like hot garbage and want to go home, change into leggings, and watch *The X Files* for about 30 hours.

But Logan strides into my office and tells me we have to go to Bridges and Bitters. When I shake my head, she leans across my desk. "Remember a few years ago when I wanted to go crawl in a hole or move back to my hometown and live with my mother?" I shake my head again. "Yes, you do. I know you remember how you showed up at my office and dragged me to a Foof meeting and changed my life."

I purse my lips. "My life has already changed," I tell her. I gesture around the room. "I have everything I ever wanted."

She crosses her arms and glares at me. "No, Samantha. No you don't. Come on." She physically hoists me from my chair and walks me down the hall.

"I don't want to ride in that ridiculous jalopy your boyfriend drives."

She laughs. "That's a cheap shot, madam. You know he's my fiancé now." She hustles me outside and into one of the giant white buses I had reserved for AJ's students. I really can't seem to get away from him, or rather the memories of chasing after him in hopes of…what? What did I expect from him other than what he gave me. How did he phrase it? Good dick.

That's all I have mental space for anyway. I'm not sure why I'm this worked up about it going away. I sink into the first seat behind the driver as the entire staff loads into the bus. I perk up when some of the developers climb aboard, waving at me.

When we get to Bridges and Bitters, Esther greets us with a tray of fragrant drinks. She sets the tray on a table and points at me. "This girl is on fire," she shouts, and lights the tray of drinks with a match as the Alicia Keys song blasts from the sound system. My staff bursts into applause.

I have to admit this is an amazing greeting. And by admit, I mean I start crying. Esther rushes around the table and pulls me into a hug. "Sam, come on. I told you it's apple cider season. Are you sad your special drink isn't pumpkin spice?"

That makes me laugh and I shake my head. "Apple cider is perfect, Esther. Thank you."

Logan wheedles her way into the hug. "Esther told me about the grand entrance and I was a little worried. But…it's really true, Sam. You're on fire! You're a fucking smash hit."

I gasp. "Logan, I didn't think you used language like that." We both laugh and I sip the cocktail, a mix of Fireball whisky, hard apple cider, and true love from my true friends. "I was told there'd be cakes?"

Esther gestures toward the bar, where there's a display of tiny, decadent desserts from Le Beau Gateau. "You've got a choice between bete noir, lemon cake, and burnt almond torte." Seeing my face, Esther laughs and hands me a plate. "Or take one of each. It's your party!"

I do just that and park myself in a cozy booth with cake and whisky, watching wistfully as my entire staff gets hammered.

Only it's not just my staff. I look around, confused. My friends are all here. All of them. All the Brady ladies, all the Stag ladies, Esther, Chloe, Piper…we haven't had a full Foof showing like this since Orla's baby shower. Every woman is beaming and shaking a shiny green pompon. "Samantha Vine! You did it!" Nicole smacks a kiss on my lips and hip checks me. "You're all over the news."

Orla scowls as Esther hands her a cocktail. "Why do you look like that?" She glances at Logan, still holding on to my arm. "Why does she look like her rabbit has pinkeye?"

And then something terrible happens. I start to cry.

"Oh, hell," Esther says. She puts the whiskey down on the bar and walks around. She wraps me in a firm hug and pats my hair and I don't know why I'm crying, but I definitely get mascara tears all over her shirt.

After a few minutes of this Esther guides me down the hall to the meeting room where we usually gather so the regular patrons don't have to endure our cackling. It's mostly me cackling, usually.

With a gentle nudge, Esther pushes me into the chaise lounge and I sigh. As she sits beside me I see that everyone else has followed her in, with Celeste bringing up the rear carrying a tray of snacks. I smile at that. She's really leaning in to being a mom and grandma these days.

"Tell us what happened," Esther says.

My lip wavers as I look around the room, at all these women I fiercely defend on the regular. All these women who have offered me advice every step of the way as I launched Vinea from nothing. "I should feel happy," I tell them. "I just reached the pinnacle of success in my business."

"Damn right you did." Nicole pumps her fist in the air.

I shake my head. "I realized the other day that…I don't like what I'm doing anymore." I think about all the time I spent this past month reassuring board members that our work was the same it has always been. That our product has not changed in its usefulness. "I'm just not cut out to be a figurehead like this." I shake my hands in the air. "It all feels like constant bullshit and all I want to do is talk about data and stretch my fingers over a really tricky data correlation map."

Piper smiles. "I know a little bit about how it feels when your dream job doesn't turn out quite how you imagined it." Logan grunts her agreement. "Sweetie, it's okay to change your goals."

I scrunch up my face. "I don't think my goals are different. I want Vinea to be everywhere. I want everyone to be able to access this software, to collaborate and share data and change the shape of research." I take a swig of the signature cocktail Celeste offers. "This is really good."

Esther squeezes my leg. "I splurged for you, friend. You're worth it."

I shake my head. "You shouldn't have done that."

She recoils. "What the hell do you mean? You're the most supportive Foof in this whole group. You've been fresh out of fucks longer than anyone else here."

"Ha!" I shake my head. "It's all a lie. I have so many fucks, Esther." I hiccup. "So many."

Orla says, "Why don't you tell us a little bit about your fucks and we'll see how we can help you release them."

Everyone nods and so I take a deep breath and I tell them about my family. How I can't seem to stop doing everything for them despite their utter lack of appreciation for that effort. "And now work is starting to feel a little bit like that. A huge responsibility I wasn't expecting to take on…" I take a huge, shaky inhale. "And when I stopped just once to do something nice for myself, it all turned to shit and he yelled at me and said I was using him."

I start sobbing again as my friends stroke my hair and rub my arms. I'm not sure who all steps in to support me, but when I open my eyes again I see a sea of faces in front of me, looking concerned. Nicole pats my leg. "Tell me who we need to kill, Sam. I have pregnant lady hormones and I'm not afraid to use them."

I whimper a little and give them a summary of how AJ assumed I disseminated the thank-you video from his students. How he accused me of being nice to them to gain positive press. "And then he acted like he was just giving me sex to be nice to me or something."

At this, the Foof members collectively gasp and Esther smashes a bottle against the table. She brandishes the jagged neck. "Let me at him," she says. "I stood up for him!"

I shake my head. "He really did give me good sex."

Celeste taps her nails on the wooden table and scrunches up her face. "You know what I think?"

I shake my head. "No, but I'd love to hear."

She nods. "I think you should be so proud of yourself, honey. You did all this." She gestures around the room. "You made this group for all these women! You've all done so much for each other. And you built that whole company to boot."

"Hear, hear!" Juniper raises her glass and smacks the table.

Celeste nods. "I watched my husband and then my son deal with jobs that made them miserable, with people who made them cringe." She shrugs. "Life is too short for either of those things." She walks over to me and squeezes my shoulder. "Let's celebrate today's success, send you to bed, and get you a career coach tomorrow."

Nicole perks up. "I love this advice," she says. "Who do we know who coaches high power executives?"

Maddie and Emma trade glances and everyone starts murmuring, trying to think of someone to help me sort out my feelings about work. I sip my drink and stare at my friends, loving them all so much I don't know what to do apart from try to buy them anything their hearts desire.

"But guys," I say, waiting until the din dies down. "What the hell do I do about AJ?"

Esther snorts. "Fuck him."

I sob-laugh. "I want to! I really, really want to…"

Orla shakes her head. "Huh-uh. He's gonna need to grovel before that can happen."

Logan nods. "Big time. Nobody says mean things about my boss."

I let out a final long moan and I really do feel a little better about everything when I'm done. "You guys are the best thing in my life," I tell them.

Chloe leans in for a hug and kisses me on the forehead. "Right   back   at   you,   sweetie."

CHAPTER THIRTY-THREE

AJ

I pat Margot's hand as we sit in the chairs outside the principal's office. "Ms. Vinelli won't be angry," I assure her.

Margot's eyes widen. "She's never mad," she says. "I just don't want anyone to be disappointed."

"Oh, Margot, nobody is disappointed in you." My heart surges at the thought of her anxiety about this. "This is a problem for adults to manage. For instance, I should have monitored the tablet devices' ability to access the internet…"

I'm cut off by our principal opening her office door, setting off a series of tinkling door chimes. "Mr. Trachtenberg! Ms. Costa! Please, come in!" Margot hops up and walks into the office, familiarly taking a seat in a papasan chair and squeezing a fuzzy throw pillow onto her lap.

I follow less enthusiastically and perch on the edge of a folding chair. Kellie Vinelli sinks into her white chair and drapes her arms over the arm-rests. "Now," she says, smiling as ever. "Who can tell me why I've asked you to come here today?"

I roll my eyes and stifle a groan. "I know my students were pictured in a video recorded during my class, and that the video is circulating the web." She opens her mouth and I hold up a finger. "I also know we didn't get photo and media release forms from all the kids' guardians this year and that we are not allowed to have such a video circulating the web."

Kellie Vinelli smiles and steeples her fingers on her lap. "That's about the gist of things. Very good, Mr. Trachtenberg."

Margot starts squirming in her seat and finally bursts out, "It was my fault. I encouraged everyone to make the video. At first we just emailed it to Ms. Vine to thank her for the field trip! But then it was my idea to expand it and post it online." Her cheeks flush. Kellie nods as she speaks and opens her own mouth to reply when Margot jumps to her feet. "I just got the best idea." She claps her hands. "Mr. T, what if we call all the adults and ask them to send in their forms?"

I groan audibly this time. Half my students' parents and guardians haven't listed active phone numbers. Ms. Vinelli taps her chin with a manicured nail. "May I see the video in question?"

I furrow my brow at her, incredulous that she hasn't even seen the thing and yet she sent schoolwide memos about it, complete with her signature exclamation points. But Margot is unperturbed, rummaging in her bag for her Vinea-issued tablet. I cede a mental point to the principal's genius when I observe her studying the lack of security to access the device and open some of the apps. My stomach turns at the thought of how much worse things could have been than the students posting a positive video.

As Margot plays the video, Kellie notes the students whose faces are visible: only five, including Margot.

When the video stops, Kellie sighs. "Well, Margot, we do know your mother gave permission for us to use your picture."

Margot grins. "One down, four to go, right?"

Kellie nods. "Why don't you head on to class, dear? Mr. Trachtenberg and I will discuss some of the specifics of this growth opportunity."

Margot nods and heads out of the room, looking relieved. I

ease up at her change in demeanor. I can handle a consequence. I just don't want my middle schoolers to feel discouraged. When the office door clicks shut again in another tinkle of chimes, Kellie adopts a more relaxed posture. "AJ. Adriel. You know, I'm not sure which you prefer?"

"AJ is fine."

"Do you have contact information for the other four students who appear in that video?" She raises a brow and points to the list on her desk.

I nod. "Some of them. Between me and Leo I bet we can at least make contact."

Kellie bites her lip. "I'm sure you know I need you to collect the tablets so the district IT staff can set up security features." I nod again. She smiles, back to her cheery demeanor. "Excellent! So you'll deposit the devices with my admin by end of day and retroactively get me those release forms! Wasn't it so good to catch up?"

My eyes widen as I realize I'm being dismissed.

I hide in my classroom during my prep period, too overwhelmed to go and get my lunch from the teachers' lounge. I'm not surprised when I hear a tap on my classroom door, however, and look up to see Leo. He slides into the room and closes the door behind him. "Want to tell me why I just got a memo to collect the students' tablet devices?"

I blow a raspberry. "Did you know they all have social media apps on them? And that the students have been faking older birthdays to access them?"

Leo winces. "Whoops."

I snort. "Yeah. Whoops. I managed to get 18 from my first class. Two of the kids said they left theirs at home. They all moaned that they won't even be fun anymore by the time we give them back."

Leo perches on the edge of my desk. "This is all your

fault," he deadpans. I smack his leg. "Well," he says, crossing his arms, "what's with the data analysis bird thingy you brought up at the staff meeting. Will they be able to access that on the locked down, no-fun tablets?"

I nod. "Should be able to." I flip open my laptop, intending to show him the website where Samantha made the rough section for the kids to collect data on the chimney swift migrations. "The kids can join local researchers tracking frog populations, owl hoots, lots of different things throughout the city." I pause while the site loads. "Hell, we can walk right over to Frick Park to do all this and still use the school wifi to enter the data." The page opens with a fluttering bird animation. I feel a lump form in my throat when I see that she fine-tuned the whole thing, making it look professional and organized, adding tabs for other citizen science projects all suitable for middle schoolers to use. I turn to Leo. "I'm such an asshole," I whisper.

He nods. "I know, AJ. It's okay."

"She really does just want to help people," I mutter. Leo continues nodding. "I fucked up with her, Leo. What do I do?"

He grips my shoulders. "You need to go apologize." He nods his head toward the door. "Go on. I've got prep last period today. I'll cover your class."

I feel my heart race and I shake my head. "I need to clean up my mess here first."

Leo grins. "You don't think I can collect some iPads from your damn honor students? They probably already heard the rumor and turned them in downstairs. These little weasels will do anything to avoid getting in trouble."

I grab my keys from my desk drawer and stuff them in my pocket. "Thank you, Leo. Seriously."

"Any time, man. Now think big with that apology, AJ. And then   go   bigger   than   that."

CHAPTER THIRTY-FOUR
Samantha

Logan steps into the conference room and claps her hands. "Today is a good day, buddy. We did it!"

I smile at her. It's been a whirlwind for sure. Even my father called to acknowledge that he read about the public offering, which is about the closest he comes to telling me he feels proud.

The past few nights, instead of running around drinking with my team, I curled up on my couch and kept coding the data entry pages for AJ's nature projects. I even did some digging and found some other local projects that could use a similar data entry page, so I got all that loaded on the site. I smile, thinking about Margot maybe doing a data plot this summer after all the students chart the birds using the towers in the city parks.

Audrey pecks me on the cheek, drawing my attention back to the moment. "Look," she says, "I know you're wiped out. It's been a heck of a haul getting to this point." She claps her hands. "Which is why I'm sending you home. As Chief of Staff, I can make these kinds of decisions."

Shane gives her a thumbs up. I shake my head. "I can't go home. I'm in charge here."

Logan pats my shoulder. "You are in charge. It's your company and you can do whatever the fuck you want.

Weren't those your words?"

"You can't hold me accountable for things I said when I was drunk on Fireball."

Another pat from Logan. "Come on, babe. Let me call you a ride home. You're beat." I sigh and let her guide me outside. She's right—I am exhausted. This week in particular has felt a month long. We get to the parking lot and for a second, I think I see AJ standing there. I rub my eyes, but when I pop them open again, he's still there. In fact, he makes eye contact with me and strides in my direction.

I shake my head. "Nope," I say, spinning on my heel. "You had your turn." AJ's eyes are intense as he stares at me from beneath a fringe of dark hair.

By this point, Logan and Audrey have noticed AJ and look concerned. "What's going on out here?" Logan frowns.

AJ wrings his hands as he looks me in the eye. "I owe you an apology. I owe you so much more than an apology. My students posted that video online themselves and I jumped to conclusions about you, Samantha."

"Figures," I mutter. I take a deep breath. "I'm used to people assuming the worst about me. You've read the news lately, right?"

Logan and Audrey back away. "We'll be inside if you need us, Sam." I close my eyes and nod, listening to their retreating footsteps. I feel so relieved to see him, to hear him admitting he was wrong, that I worry I still might be dreaming.

"Walk with me?" He gestures away from my office building, toward the bicycle path along the river. I follow him and sink onto a stone bench overlooking the Allegheny.

He sits next to me and squeezes his legs with his hands. "I wasn't fair to you. You kept showing me who you were, who you are. And I kept not believing you."

I huff, letting out a little of my frustrations with him. "Well, it's for the best anyway. I would have just gotten attached and then you'd go off and die on me." He pulls his head back and I stare at him. "Oh, aren't we both exploring how our past wounds impact our relationships? My bad." After my Foof crew suggested a career coach, I had an introductory session with a woman who is a licensed therapist specializing in helping executives meet their goals. We talked a ton about my mom. I might have also unloaded to her about AJ.

"Well I have no intention of dying anytime soon, unless it's possible to burn up from shame." He looks at a trio of kayakers paddling past. "You're right that I have old wounds I need to address." He rakes a hand through his hair. "I let myself believe the worst about you because I couldn't let myself believe you see the best in me."

I stare out at the water. "You brought me tacos," I mutter. "Do you know how few people I let realize I need help remembering to eat?"

"If I promise to never take that privilege for granted ever again, could I maybe bring you tacos tomorrow?" I shake my head no. His face sags. "Okay. That's fair. Thank you for letting me apologize, anyway."

"I'm busy tomorrow," I tell him, pressing my lips together briefly. "I have to go count chimney swifts at the park with some teenagers."

AJ breaks into a grin and slides closer to me on the bench. He reaches for my hand and pulls it to his chest. "I swear, Samantha, they would vaporize in a haze of Axe body spray if you showed up while they were counting birds."

I nod. "We'd have to record that as a weather event on the form."

AJ smiles and leans his forehead against mine. His warmth fills the space around me and I feel like I want to cry again. My emotions are all over the place today. "I'd ask if I could kiss you here, but I'm afraid your staff is standing at the window waiting to put us on Instagram."

I laugh and lean closer to him, savoring his scent. "Well

then you better take me somewhere else to kiss me, Adriel."

CHAPTER THIRTY-FIVE

AJ

Samantha tells me she's way too tired to walk all the way to her car and asks me to kayak her home. I laugh and offer her a piggy-back ride instead. "You're no fun," she pouts, but laughs when I stoop and ease her up onto my back, skirt be damned.

"We've already established that," I tell her, hiking her up higher and squeezing her thighs as she grips my neck. "Are you drunk? Am I taking advantage of you?"

Sam cackles. "You better take advantage of me, Trachtenberg. I was promised some extensive groveling."

When we reach my car, I lower her to the ground and help her inside the passenger seat. As I walk around to the drivers side, reaching for the gear shift, I finally understand why people enjoy driving an automatic. I have to keep my hand away from her to downshift at every traffic light. Samantha stares at me quietly while I drive. I speed up to catch the next light when it's yellow and she cheers. She looks confused when I pull up outside of my building in Squirrel Hill. "Where the hell are you taking me?"

I shrug. "My place. I can take you to yours if you'd rather?"

She shakes her head. "No, this is fine. I want to see where you live."

I rush around to open her door and help her to her feet. "Let's get something clear." I clasp her hands. "This apartment is where I've been wallowing. You bring me to life, Samantha Vine."

"Well that's a really nice thing to say." Her lip quivers and I lean to kiss her, giving her ass a squeeze to try and lighten the mood after revealing something so heavy. I guide her inside the building, up the stairs, and inside my door, where she stops to laugh incredulously. "This is your home? Did you just move in? Why don't you have any possessions?"

She paces around the room, her footsteps echoing in the near-empty space. "I can't deal with this. Honey, I'm going to need to take you shopping for furniture. And decorations. At minimum a portrait of me…"

I step close to her and nibble her earlobe. "I like the idea of that," I tell her. "But there is one essential piece of furniture here that I'd like to show you right now."

"What's that? A concrete block bookshelf?"

She squeaks when I give her a gentle shove down the hall. She laughs when she sees my bed, just a mattress and box spring on the tiny metal frame that came with it from the store. I flick on the overhead light, squint up at the fluorescent glare, and decide I can make do with the glow from the hall light. "Let's get you naked," I tell her.

She bites her lip. "Am I going to get to stroke your pelt?"

I nod, kneeling in front of her to help her out of her leggings and ankle boots. "I certainly hope so." Samantha lifts her dress over her head and sits on the bed, naked apart from a dark green bra and matching panties. "You're a goddess," I whisper, letting my fingertips skate along her body. "I've been such a fool."

"Mmm, this is an excellent early grovel." She reaches behind her back to unhook her bra and tosses it over my shoulder. "I'm going to need to see more man-bear, please." I chuckle and start to undress, pausing frequently to kiss and pet her. Samantha coos when I finally take off my undershirt. I've never had a woman so excited by my body hair. I should have taken that as a sign early on. I sigh, reminded again that I have some atonement to achieve tonight.

Kissing my way up her body, I climb on top of Samantha, who wriggles beneath me like she's trying to burrow into my stomach. Her movements turn to rolling hips and her coos turn to breathy sighs as I slide downward, licking my way along her silky skin until I hook my teeth around the waistband of her panties.

Once we're both fully nude, I pause to admire how we look together. She seems to shine in the shitty light of my apartment and I nearly disappear in the darkness, except for the fierce erection that points straight out toward Samantha. Like a compass guiding me toward true north, my dick twitches until I settle myself between her thighs.

"This feels so nice," she says. "I love the weight of you on top of me."

"Mmm." I massage her breasts, lapping at her nipples and delighting in watching them pucker and tighten for me. I reach downward, finding slick heat in start contrast to the firm points on her chest. Sam's mouth drops open and her head falls back as I stroke her, as I reach inside and find her soft and warm and wanting.

"Sam," I whisper, kissing her navel. "Do you want to use a condom?" I lick a line back up to her breast before adding, "I've had a physical recently…"

She blows out a breath as I twirl my finger inside her. "I'm…oooh, that's good. I'm good. On pill. Ahhh!" I tap on her clit as I think about what we've just decided, that I'm about to slide my naked cock inside her body with no barrier. Just the two of us, as close as it's possible to be, gliding together toward shared pleasure.

"I want you so much," I tell her. "I've always wanted you. From the first moment I saw you."

Sam lifts up so she's resting on her elbows, staring at me. "I've been hot for teacher since day one. But can we talk about that later?" She juts her hips up from the bed to emphasize her point. "We're celebrating 16 million shares here, remember?"

"Damn right," I say, pressing a thumb into her clit and loving the view as she arches back, groaning at my touch. I circle her pleasure zone a few times until I feel her starting to clench around the finger sliding in and out of her body. I adjust my weight, redouble my efforts, and add in a tongue circling her right nipple until I feel Samantha give me what I want: her release.

"AJ!" She shrieks my name as her hips jerk beneath me. Her arousal fills my nostrils and I can't take it anymore. I have to be inside her, to feel her throbbing and pulsing. And so I take what she's offering. I use one hand to line up the tip of my cock and I slide into paradise.

Both of us groan at the smooth fit, at the feel of us coming together. "I'm so full of you," Sam pants, rolling her hips and lifting to grind against me as the final waves of her orgasm subside. "I love it," she purrs. "Oh, I love this."

"So good," I groan, and then I bark out a laugh when she tugs on my chest hair before digging her nails into my ass. I love this about being with her—she surprises me every moment. Nothing about her is what I expect and…that's the beauty of being with her. She drags me right outside my comfort zone and then lights my comfort zone on fire. "I can't get enough."

Letting go of my ass, Samantha grabs my head and kisses me. I taste the cinnamon whiskey on her tongue. I taste her success and her pain, and I want to be here for all of it, standing by her side, wrapping her in my furry limbs, doing what I can to support her. "Samantha." Her name is a prayer as I move inside her.

"Adriel!" I hear the desperation in her voice and I know

she's close. I know we're about to topple over the edge together. She wraps her legs around my hips, pulling me deeper, closer, locking us tighter together. This is where I want to stay, always. If she'll have me.

"I need you," she moans. "Please! Please!" I don't know how to give her what she wants, not consciously. But as I study her face and read the roll of her body beneath me, I respond with my touch. One thrust, one stroke, one pinch, and she clamps around my cock. "Yes. Yes, just like that," Sam moans, a contented smile on her face as she comes. And then I'm chasing right behind her, firing inside her with a force that leaves me breathless.

Catching my breath, I collapse in her arms, resting my head on the pillow beside hers. I look into her eyes, feeling perfectly happy. So safe, so content.

"Now that's a good grovel," she whispers, tracing her nails along my spine.

"Thank you," I murmur. "Happy to oblige."

CHAPTER THIRTY-SIX
Samantha

I'm so late. Inexcusably late. "AJ?" I holler into the cavernous bunker he calls an apartment. No answer. "Adriel? Mr. T?" Shit. Did he really leave without me? I set my floppy hat on his kitchen counter and reach for my phone. I'm supposed to walk over to Blue Slide Park with him to meet up with his students. We installed a new chimney swift tower with some help from the high school wood shop students, and the local bird experts think some swifts will roost in it tonight.

But things ran late at work today.

When I check my phone, I don't see any missed messages from him. I bite my lip, not sure if I should call him or just head over to Beechwood Blvd on my own. Just as I decide to lace up my hiking boots myself, I hear the jingle of keys in his front door. "Sam!" His voice is frantic and he rushes in the door, yanking off his tie and sweater vest. "Oh, good, you're still here. I'm so late."

I stare at him in disbelief. "Adriel Trachtenberg, you're never late. Are you...disheveled right now?" He waves a hand and streaks past me, stripping off his teacher clothes and leaving them in heaps on the floor. I am deeply aroused.

Seconds later, he dashes out of his room wearing cargo pants and a Franklin Middle School t-shirt. I swallow a thick knot and close my eyes. Now is not the time to sink to my knees and run my fingers through his leg hair. He looks at me strangely as he grabs his clipboard from his couch. "Why do you look weird? Come on." He gestures a head toward the door and I plunk my hat back on my head and trot after him.

He hurries down the steps to the ground floor and extends his hand behind him, fingers curling as they wait to clasp mine. I link my hand in his and rush to catch up. He frowns at the red light and looks both ways. "I think we can dash across," he says. I nod solemnly at Adriel Trachtenberg weighing the greater evil between jaywalking and showing up late for an extracurricular event he's leading.

As we hustle down Beechwood toward the playground entrance, I ask, "So what held you up today?"

"You first," he says, nearly tripping on the uneven sidewalk in his haste.

"Well I was on time," I assert and burst into laughter when he turns to grin at me mischievously. "Okay, I was also late. But we made the offer and Lyra accepted. She's going to start in two weeks."

"Nice!" AJ's smile is genuine and he gives my hand a squeeze. "Things didn't work out with Chloe's husband? Teddy?"

I wave a hand dismissively. "I'm sure he'd be fine, but it just felt like too much of a conflict to hire my friend's spouse."

"Hm," AJ growls. "How did he take the rejection?"

"Well, Mr. T, I'm not entirely sure." We pause at the corner and look both ways before darting across one final intersection before the park. I sigh. It took a lot of discussion and three rounds of interviews before I finally accepted that Chloe's husband is not right candidate to replace me as CEO at Vinea. But Lyra definitely is. And I hope Chloe understands that. Not gonna lie, I don't love how my friend Chloe feels a lot of the time in her marriage. But I've got my own relationship to focus on these days, and I'm learning more about how much work goes into a two-way partnership.

After a month of sessions with my new coach, I learned a lot about what I really want from my job. It literally never occurred to me that I could hire someone else to be CEO of Vinea, but now I know all about the differences between a Chief Technology Officer and a Chief Executive Officer.

As soon as I ironed all that out, I took a proposal to the board and we launched a search for someone who knows about business performance and management and all that jazz. Logan is beside herself. She won't have to explain any lingo or jargon to Lyra, Shane and Audrey can schedule meetings about meetings, and I get to focus on my true passion: our software and our tech team.

I squeeze AJ's hand again. "Now you, boo. How was your session?"

AJ smiles, a small gesture that shows me he's thinking about how to answer. "We did a lot of breath work this time." AJ has been seeing a therapist, talking a lot about how he snaps to anger so quickly, how frightened he's been of getting left again. "And then I told Naomi you're worth risking my heart."

I pull him to a stop by the wooden sign marking the park entrance, where the red leaves are floating down to the ground in the dusky pink sky. "AJ," I whisper, clutching my heart with the hand not squeezing his. "Thank you for telling me that." I press a palm to his cheek. "And I'm not going anywhere."

He nods. "I think I know that now." He leans in to kiss me, but we are interrupted by whoops and whistles. I peek over his shoulder to see a cluster of seventh graders, some of whom are filming us with their cellphones.

"Yo, Mr. T, this will be great footage for our YouTube channel. Slip her some tongue."

AJ frowns and shakes his head. "Jayden, you know I'll

never approve that sort of content on our school channel."

Jayden winks and slips his phone in his pocket. "Just playin, Mr. T. But you and Ms. Vine better hurry. The bird guy says we can go count owl hoots as soon as the sun sets." He and AJ's students wander down the path toward the wooden tower, where they've laid out a few blankets and milk crates. A Citiparks employee gives us a wave and gestures toward the sky.

As AJ tugs me onto his lap on a plaid blanket, a murmur of delight goes up from the crowd of teens and onlookers. The chimney swifts swirl through the sunset in a spiral and AJ traces a matching pattern on my back with his finger. I hear Maya and Dante counting the birds and filming the synchronized swoops and dips from the flock, but it's hard for me to concentrate on anything other than the soft tickle of AJ's breath against my ear.

"I'm so thankful you stalked me," he whispers. I turn to face him, narrowing my eyes at his interpretation of our meet cute. He shrugs.

I flick his nose. "It would have been easier if your voicemail message wasn't so weird."

He grins and presses his forehead against mine. "I was going for intrigue," he says, kissing me briefly and then remembering that we're surrounded by children. Technically the Citiparks ranger is in charge tonight, but we still shouldn't be making out in front of kids with video cameras. "I think my vocal stylings landed me a pretty hot babe."

I sigh and lean back against his chest. "I will accept your hot babe assessment."

"Good," he whispers. We watch as the sun sets, the birds roost and the program shifts to one of quiet listening as the ranger models the calls of different owls living in the park. A haunting cry emerges from a nearby tree and AJ's hands squeeze me as he communicates that he hears it, too.

We listen for a bit longer and the students record their

observations before dashing off to meet their rides or catch their buses. Soon, it's just us, alone under the stars in the crisp autumn air.

I turn in AJ's arms so I can see his eyes in the moonlight, and I feel a little swoony with the romance of it all. "You brought me on a data observation session," I tell him.

He nods and kisses my hand. "And *you* enjoy learning about science with my students."

I nod and kiss him on the mouth. "You should take me home and do other things I enjoy."

I move to stand but he tugs me back onto his lap. He holds my gaze. "I meant what I said earlier, Samantha. You're worth every risk. You're worth everything to me." He swallows. "I need to tell you I love you."

I have to check to see if the sun rose already or if the burning glow I feel is coming from inside my chest. "You love me?"

He nods. "I really do." For so long, I thought love wasn't an option for me, that I chose my work and I felt okay about that because I could make an impact that way. But here, in this park with this man who fights with me and knows what makes me tick, here under the starlight I realize it's not an either-or situation. I can rock my career and there's still enough of me leftover to matter to someone else. Someone who matters to me.

Tears well up in my eyes as I lean into the sincerity and vulnerability AJ showed me today. "I love you, too." And the two of us smile, settling in to this new reality. But it's not new, not really. This connection has been building between us for months. We both just needed to open our eyes and acknowledge it.

"Let's go inside," AJ says, shivering a bit in the cold.

I run my hands along his legs where they're bent on either side of my hips. "Yes, let's," I tell him. But neither of us moves. We sit in the park, with the owls hooting around us,

savoring the first day we were each brave enough to admit we
were   in   love.

Epilogue: Samantha

Foof is out in force this week because Chloe is about to release another book, Piper is thinking of changing jobs, and Orla is considering having a third baby. There's a *lot* to talk about, even for women who know how to keep things snappy. "I can only stay for a bit today," I tell them. "I feel bad."

Esther pulls back the drink she was about to hand me and shakes her head. "No booze until you tell us why you have to leave."

I grin. "You all know damn well it's AJ's family's Hanukkah party tonight." I tuck my hair behind my ears as my friends burst into a chorus of *awww*. "They said I can light the candle." I was able to sneak away from work for the beginning of the Foof meeting today. Sneak is the wrong word. I could leave at the end of the business day because in my new role, I don't spend my evenings sifting through paperwork I hate. These days, I strategize about new tech, fine-tune our existing tech, and sometimes sit alongside our developers to troubleshoot bugs in our products. And I freaking love it.

"Orla, do you need me to go through some of our research data to assess parental stress levels when families have more than two babies? You know I could get you a report in minutes, sweetie." She shakes her head. "It was more of a passing idea than a real thing I want to try," she says, bouncing Nicole's baby on her hip. "Besides, with this one, I can cuddle him and hand him right on back to his mama."

Nicole shakes her head, happy to have help with her infant. Seeing the Brady family ladies reminds me of my own family obligations for the evening, so I excuse myself and bundle up for the drive to AJ's parents' house. He's meeting me there after work, since his students are finishing up a research project and staying late with him at the middle school.

I arrive before he does, and Avi tugs me in the door in a big hug. "Sam! We're so glad to have you here tonight." I peek over her shoulder to see AJ's parents and Bubbie grinning and munching on cheese and crackers. AJ's grandmother sees me and claps her hands. I swear, they like me better than they do AJ, and I don't mind it a bit.

Avi takes my coat and hands me a glass of wine, and when AJ arrives a few minutes later, I laugh because he has to hang his own coat and pour his own drink. He snuggles up to my side, pressing a cold kiss to my neck. "You smell like snow," I whisper to him. "Does that smell have a name, too?"

He scrunches up his face. "I'm not actually sure. I'll report back later." He taps my nose. "You ready for this?"

AJ's dad clears his throat. "I think everyone is here now. Right? Nobody else?" AJ's mom shakes her head. "Right, then. Time to get lit!"

AJ rolls his eyes. "Every year, Dad." His father shrugs as we all walk over to the picture window in the living room, where the menorah is set on the sill. "Okay," my boyfriend stands behind me. "Do you remember what to do?"

I look around at his family and nod. "We light the helper candle first and then use it to spread the light." AJ nods. My hand shakes as I try and fail to light the match and he stands behind me, pressed close as he helps me strike the match. "Want me to do it with you?" His words are soft in my ear and I nod. Together, we touch the flame to the wick and I smile as the glow fills the room.

AJ's family begins singing the prayer, and AJ's voice is

low beside me, singing along as I shake out the match and then pick up the candle, using it to light the menorah. It's such a lovely moment, full of gratitude and happiness. We all stand together in silence for a bit and AJ wraps his arms around my waist, softly kissing my head.

"All right," his mother's voice breaks the stillness. "Latke time." Avi rubs her palms together and rushes to the table.

AJ guides me into a seat beside him and says, "Okay. So I didn't prepare you for this because it really is a moment of truth. A rite of passage." Avi leans her elbows on the table. I hear Bubbie and AJ's mom stop clattering in the kitchen and they bend their heads around the door frame. AJ's dad looks anxious. "Samantha Vine, when we hand you a latke, will you top it with applesauce or sour cream?" I blink at him in confusion. He pats my leg. "Don't feel like you need to answer right away. Think about it, because your answer will determine your future with the Trachtenberg family."

Everyone laughs, including me, but I don't need to think very long. Crispy potatoes and onions? "No contest. Sour cream," I say, and then I gasp as his family groans.

AJ closes his eyes and shakes his head, pressing his hands to his heart. "Samantha," he says. "You've disappointed me deeply."

Bubbie makes a "tsk" sound and serves me a few sizzling latkes. "Adriel don't be dramatic. Some people like sour cream. Every now and again, someone likes sour cream."

"Those people are wrong, though." Avi scoops applesauce onto her plate from a serving dish on the table.

I bite my lip and stare at the Trachtenberg family. "You know, I could pop open a data collection module, chart some nationwide or even global latke topping preferences?"

AJ leans forward and kisses me on the forehead. "I love you, Samantha."

"I love you, too. Do you want me to run a program? It won't take long…"

AJ shakes his head. "I love you, but it's not necessary to run a model."

"Well why not? Surely you'd want to know if your family's firm belief is based in fact?" I take a bite of the latke. "Bubbie, this is amazing. Do I taste rosemary?"

She nods. "Just a pinch."

AJ continues shaking his head. "It doesn't need to be fact. It just is."

"I don't accept that answer," I tell him, wiping a dab of sour cream on his nose and laughing at his frown.

He growls and snaps his teeth at me. "Mother, you're going to have to excuse Samantha. The sour cream probably impacted her ability to think straight."

They tease me about my "faulty" preference for sour cream and joke that they're not going to buy me enough to last all eight nights. I lean against AJ and soak it all in, the bickering, the meal, the spark and glow between us.

AJ and I have done so much work over the past few months—both of us are feeling the impact our coach and therapist are having on our happiness at work and with family. I'm not flying to Virginia this year for Christmas, in fact. I'm joining my boyfriend for a day of volunteering with his synagogue right here in Pittsburgh. And then he's moving in to my townhouse on New Year's when his lease expires. He feels ready, after working to unpack his feelings…and since he spends most nights at my place anyway.

After the meal, AJ's father gets out their dreidel and AJ and his sister squabble some more over the rules of the game while I munch on the chocolate coins. I fiddle with the gold foil wrappers from the candy as AJ gets heated over one of his spins, jumping in the air and pumping his fist, knocking a tray of cookies off the edge of the table. He and I both dive for them together, scooping them up off the floor.

Laughing, AJ piles the cookies back on the tray and grins at me. "These are perfectly good," he says.

I nod. "It would be a shame to waste them." He kisses me, tasting of chocolate. Leaning in closer, he whispers, "I should probably take you home, though, so we can eat the floor cookies in private."

I grin and clutch at his hand under the tablecloth. "I like how you think."

~~~

Thank you for reading! The Bridges and Bitters series continues with **Liquid Courage**, a marriage in crisis rom-com about Chloe and her husband, Ted.

Want to see what happens next for AJ and Samantha? Click here for a steamy bonus epilogue:
  bookhip.com/RSPTLFA

Curious to learn more about Doug and his wife, Amy? Their story, Lesson Plans: An Education in Romance, is coming soon!

Author's Note

Whew, what a ride! I've had Samantha Vine knocking around inside my head since I wrote Cal and Logan's book, Vibration, well over a year ago. Never in a million years did I think it would take me this long to bring Fireball to market, but here we are. Pandemic has impacted me in unexpected waves, and the disruption of early 2022 really made it hard for me to write rom-com.

But I was always planning to give Samantha her own book. As soon as I figured out the woman for Cal, I knew she'd need a group of women to support her when she moved to Pittsburgh, and the idea for the Bridges and Bitters series really fell into place as I thought about how important found family is for people who (for many reasons) can't access their family-family.

I didn't know who her hero would be, though, until I saw a meme about how Alan Alda met his wife. They were at a dinner party, where the host dropped dessert on the ground. Most of the guests agreed that the dessert was trashed, but Alan and his wife shared the floor cake and the rest was history. And then I knew—Samantha Vine needed a man who would eat floor cake with her. The rest of the story fell into place pretty easily from there.

Thank you all so much for your patience as I worked on this story, canceled its release, worked on it some more, and finally brought it to your hands. Your support throughout this process has meant the world to me. I'm deep into my research for Chloe's book now. Stay tuned!

~Lainey